SECOND CHANCE

W. STONE COTTER

SECOND CHANCE

GODWIN BOOKS

HENRY HOLT AND COMPANY

NEW YORK

Henry Holt and Company, *Publishers since 1866*
Henry Holt® is a registered trademark of Macmillan Publishing Group, LLC
120 Broadway, New York, New York 10271 • mackids.com

Library of Congress Control Number: 2019951486
ISBN 978-1-62779-259-2

Our books may be purchased in bulk for promotional, educational,
or business use. Please contact your local bookseller or the
Macmillan Corporate and Premium Sales Department at (800) 221-7945
ext. 5442 or by email at MacmillanSpecialMarkets@macmillan.com.

First edition, 2021 / Series design by April Ward
Printed in the United States of America by LSC Communications,
Harrisonburg, Virginia

1   3   5   7   9   10   8   6   4   2

This book is dedicated to my brilliant and indomitable
nephews, Bobby, Jack Henry, Will, and Ben

And to Krissy Olson, my one true love forever

CHAPTER 1

On the ninth of August, at 3:47 p.m., the thermometer in the little town of Starling, Texas, reached 115 degrees Fahrenheit, the hottest moment so far this year, and the Jeopard siblings, Pauline and Chance, found themselves trapped indoors with their mother, Daisy, and her new friend, Neville Fred Antaso. They were all sitting around the living room in the air-conditioning like exhausted, over-fed felines, waiting for the temperature to drop.

Boring.

Life in general had been rather boring since Pauline and Chance had escaped from Saint Philomene's Infirmary, deep below the Earth's surface, at the beginning of the summer. Nothing aboveground could compare to their harrowing days underground, and they—Pauline, Chance, and their dear friend Mersey Marsh—had had to keep it all a secret from everyone they knew, though Chance had privately written and illustrated a book about their experiences. Their adventures had bound them ever closer as friends, and they met every day and talked about the perils of June.

But there was only so much to talk about, and as the endless, scorching Texas summer dragged on, the friends saw less and less of one another, and found themselves immersed in other interests. Mersey Marsh had begun dating a nice boy, Killiam Ng, Pauline had become deeply involved in her arrowhead project, and Chance was building a counterpoise trebuchet in an abandoned lot a few blocks from the house.

"How's that launcher coming along, lad?" said Fred, directing the flow of air-conditioner air with the sports section of the Starling *Town Crier*.

Chance had found the plans for the trebuchet on the internet. It was ambitious. When completed, it would throw a fifteen-pound bowling ball three hundred yards. At first Chance had been disappointed—he'd wanted a contraption that would hurl a human half a mile. But those devices were built by corporations with reinforced steel and six-digit budgets, not twelve-year-olds with power drills and scavenged two-by-fours. Fred had offered to loan Chance whatever

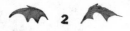

tools he needed if he could secure the materials. With his meager earnings from mowing lawns, doing chores for his mother and his neighbor, Mrs. Applebaker, along with diligent searching around town and on the neighborhood listserv, Chance was by increments acquiring materials to build his towering medieval catapult. He had already put together the base and frame assembly, and wanted nothing more than to work on it today, but 115 degrees were even too much for sun-bleached Chance Jeopard.

"Pretty good, sir," said Chance. "I still need to find something to use for the main throwing arm."

"I have a property near Chamberlain," said Fred, who had migrated to the kitchen and was mixing himself an Arnold Palmer. "It has a bunch of antique telegraph poles running through it. Maybe I could have one of my men uproot one for you. They run a good twenty feet in height. Would that do ya?"

"It sure would! That would be great, sir!"

Fred Antaso, who liked to wear pink or green guayabera shirts and razor-creased pastel golf pants, was tanned to the color of turmeric and reminded Chance of a cross between Billy Bob Thornton and a tangerine Popsicle. Chance liked Fred. Even Pauline liked Fred. He and Pauline had gone out arrowhead hunting once, and he had kept up with her for six hours in the August sun, finding a fragment of an ax-head and a small but nearly pristine Clovis point, both of which he gave her for her collection. He had further impressed her

by knapping a perfect spearhead out of a chunk of obsidian, right in the backyard.

Their mother, Daisy, had met Fred Antaso at a yoga retreat in Northampton, Massachusetts, and when they discovered they lived in neighboring towns—he in McCandless, only a mile away—they decided they would get together and practice yoga on a regular basis when they got home. It wasn't long before they were an item. It did not hurt that Fred seemed to love her children.

Yes, everyone seemed to love Neville Fred Antaso.

Except a certain somebody.

Tikki-tik-tik-tik—Mersey Marsh's long, black-painted fingernails tapped on the stained-glass window in the front door. Daisy answered.

"Mersey! Come in before you melt, heavens. Where's Killiam?"

"Diving again."

Mersey's boyfriend was a champion diver, and much of his time was spent doing just that.

"Hi, Mersey," said Chance, who was lying on the living room floor working on a 1:8 scale drawing of his trebuchet on a piece of poster board.

"Hi, Mersey," said Pauline, who was sitting in the Eames chair reading about the Gault Clovis site on her laptop.

"Hi, Mersey!" said Fred, who was sitting on the couch watching golf on TV, his Arnold Palmer sweating down his wrist.

4

"Hello," said Mersey, who stood in the middle of the room, her arms crossed, perspiring from the two-block walk from her house, strands of her midnight hair stuck to her forehead. She looked like she had something to say, but she kept her lips pursed shut. Daisy brought her an Arnold Palmer.

"Thank you."

A cheer rose up from the crowd on TV; somebody'd birdied.

"Attaboy!" shouted Fred, spilling his beverage.

Mersey Marsh seemed to be growing peeved. One brow was arched high into her bangs, one foot, shod in a black witch's shoe, tapped impatiently. She suddenly drank her Arnie in two gulps, strode over to the sink, washed out the glass, placed it in the strainer, then, in a strident, command-ing voice, boomed:

"Jeopard siblings, upstairs, now!"

Pauline and Chance leaped up. Chance grabbed a bag of gummi spiders off the kitchen counter, Pauline a beef jerky, and they both followed Mersey upstairs. The siblings arranged themselves on Pauline's bed, struggled a moment opening their snacks, then waited.

"What is it?" said Chance. Mersey always made Chance feel a little funny, as though he were suspended in a sensory-deprivation tank full of lemon Jell-O. It was not an altogether unpleasant sensation, though one he did not understand at all. When Mersey was being fierce, like now, it further

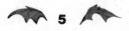

complicated his feelings. Yet he couldn't wait to see where it all was going to go. Chance felt sort of giddy.

"Yeah, what is it?" Pauline, on the other hand, was just plain curious. A fierce Mersey was a compelling Mersey. She had become rather ho-hum after taking up with that boyfriend of hers, always on about inward-twisting-tuck-and-pike armstands and other diving jargon. Pauline wanted the old Mersey back, and now Mersey stood before them, hands on her hips, a stormy look in her green eyes. Here was the Mersey she knew and loved!

"Look, you two," she said, pointing at Pauline, then at Chance, then back at Pauline. "I know how much you like old Fred Antaso—"

"And we know how much you *don't* like him," said Pauline. "So?"

"Well, I've got news for you. I've been researching him."

Mersey was a crackerjack googler. She even knew how to navigate the dark web.

"I'm not sure I want to know," said Chance, mouth full of gummi spiders.

He didn't want to find out that Fred was a retired safecracker or a bank robber who'd been on the lam for twenty years or one of the Isabella Stewart Gardner Museum thieves. Or worse. He wanted Fred Antaso to be Fred Antaso, the man who laughed at reruns of *The Love Boat* and watched golf tournaments all day and pored over Chance's trebuchet schematics.

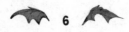

"Me neither," said Pauline, gnawing on her beef jerky. She didn't want to find out that Fred was a junk bond cheat or a crown jewel thief or a euro counterfeiter or a moonshiner. Or worse. She wanted Fred Antaso to be Fred Antaso, the man who lost spectacularly at Rummikub and Othello and Pente, who could also spot a half-buried Clovis point at twenty feet in the murk of dusk.

Pauline and Chance wanted what their mother wanted, and that was a life with Fred Antaso in it.

"Well, I'll tell you what I found out: nothing."

"Wha?"

"According to the internet," said Mersey, "there is no Neville Fred Antaso."

"What are you talking about?" said Pauline, cheeks full of jerky.

"Google returns nothing for *Neville Antaso, Antaso, Neville, Fred Antaso, Antaso, Fred, Frederick Antaso*, et cetera, et cetera, et cetera."

"So?" said Chance. "Lots of people keep a low profile."

"Not so," said Mersey. "Everyone's on the internet now. Your mom is, famous yoga impresario. Your dad, of course."

The siblings' father, Albert Wuthering Jeopard, meteorologist *extraordinaire*, had passed away only a year ago, the victim of a rogue lightning strike. The vacancy his passing had left in the family was one that no one thought could ever be filled.

Until Fred had come along.

"And you are, too, Chance," said Mersey. "When Channel Eight News did that story about you for rescuing that Samoyed from the Lonegin Creek rapids two summers ago? The news clip is on YouTube. And, Pauline, when you found acrocanthosaurus tracks and got interviewed by the Dallas Museum of Natural History? That clip is on Vimeo. I have makeup tutorials on both sites, and all of us are on Facebook. I challenge you to find someone who is not on the internet *somewhere*—a birth record, their Little League batting average, a guest at a wedding."

"But Fred . . . ," said Pauline, finishing the last of her jerky, wadding up the wrapper, and sky-hooking it into the wastebasket in the corner of her room.

"Yes. Neville Fred Antaso is absent."

"What does this mean?" Chance asked.

"I think," said Mersey, "that he's using a fake name."

"What for?" said Pauline.

"No idea," said Mersey. "What's he do, anyway?"

"Consultant," said Chance and Pauline at once.

"What does he consult, um, on?"

"Not sure," said Pauline. "Maybe oil?"

"I think cattle," said Chance. "Or stocks."

"So neither of you know."

Mersey crossed her arms, blew her bangs in the air, and looked at her friends with a mixture of compassion and vague annoyance.

"Maybe he's just a general consultant."

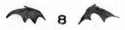

"Yeah, he knows an awful lot about everything," said Pauline.

"Could his name be an anagram?" said Chance.

"I thought of that, but the online anagram machines don't do names. I tried to work it out on paper, but couldn't come up with anything. You're both welcome to try."

CHAPTER 2

Val Sleaford, of Lubbock, Texas, had not been terribly worried when his friend and chess partner Dave Green did not answer his phone for several days earlier in the summer, but he was certainly surprised to see what bad shape Dave was in when Val knocked on his door in late June. He was shocked at the story Dave had to tell.

"You won't believe me, so I'm not even going to tell you," said Dave, opening two Dr Peppers and handing one to his friend.

"Come on," said Val, deeply curious now. Val loved a good story.

"Well," said Dave, gesturing to an easy chair. "I was sick. I was playing chess online with somebody . . . somebody who said they could cure me. *If* I followed their instructions. I wound up in a strange hospital. Underground. It was called Saint Philomene's Infirmary. They treated, strictly speaking, only nonhumans."

"Come on," said Val, sitting down in the easy chair.

"Okay, end of story."

"All right, all right, continue."

"But they could treat my illness, long story," said Dave, taking a lengthy pull on his Dr Pepper and sitting back in his chair. "I found my way there; they cured me; they sent me back. Before they did, they gave me a pill to make me forget everything I'd seen there. I faked swallowing it, spit it out later, stuck it in my pocket. So I remember everything."

"How long were you there?"

"I couldn't say; I was pretty sick. Maybe ten days. But I saw extraordinary things. Unbelievable forms of life. Strange technologies. And—I hesitate to tell *you* this—untold mineral riches."

"Is that right?"

"I saw not only the Infirmary, but outside of it, the realm of Donbaloh, as it's called. With my own eyes I saw untapped veins of palladium, emeralds, and gold."

Val Sleaford kept a straight face, but it wasn't easy. Because Val Sleaford ran one of the most aggressive and successful mining operations in all of Texas, and he was always

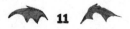

looking for somewhere new to mine. Even if Dave Green was making everything up—or had imagined everything, or dreamed it—it couldn't hurt to go looking. Stake a claim, bring a few excavators, start digging, see what happens.

"So, where is this place?"

"No idea. Texas."

"Any clues?"

"No, and if I did have a clue, I wouldn't tell you. You'd go digging the place up, Val."

It was true that *untold mineral riches* were some of Val's favorite words, but he was mainly interested in gold. Gold was what mattered in the world. Gold was in fact, as Val saw it, the problem with society. Specifically its high value. Destroy that, and you eradicate all socioeconomic ills, especially poverty. To do this, Val reasoned, one must find a vein of gold so large that its discovery would send the value of gold plummeting to nothing. Val had traveled a great deal and had seen poverty in its worst forms, from the Khayelitsha slum in Cape Town, South Africa, and the Makoko slum in Lagos, to notorious Orangi Town in Karachi, Pakistan, and the now-demolished Kowloon Walled City in Hong Kong, to the homegrown poverty of certain regions of Appalachia and the inner-city housing projects in Cleveland, New Orleans, and elsewhere. It would not be a quick fix, but Val Sleaford felt that compromising the value of gold was the answer to economic balance. Indeed, Val had written three books on the subject.

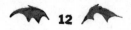

Val looked out the window. In the distance, dozens of towering wind turbines lazily spun in the incessant breeze. The joke was in this part of Texas that the wind had only ever stopped blowing once, and all the chickens fell over.

"Still have that pill?" he asked Dave Green.

Dave's eyes narrowed. He looked hard at his friend.

"Why?"

"Curious."

"I keep it in a Sucrets box."

Val thought that was quaint. He hadn't even *seen* a Sucrets box in twenty-five years. There were only Altoids boxes now. It made him feel sad for his friend.

"What else do you remember?"

"There were two human children there."

"Really."

Up until this moment Val hadn't really believed Dave. He thought he'd had some kind of fever dream or hallucination or something. But something about the detail of "two human children" had the unmistakable ring of truth.

"I was incarcerated for a while there. My cellmate, a strange creature called a Wreau, told me their names."

"Yes?"

"I'm not going to reveal them."

We'll see about that.

"Ah, yes, I understand. Say, can I use your facilities?"

"Sure."

Val returned after a few moments.

13

"Why don't you get out the chessboard?"

"It's in the back room. Just a minute."

Dave returned with his roll-up board and Staunton pieces. Val drank his Dr Pepper. Dave Green finished his. Val knew he would; Dave never left so much as a drop in a bottle of Dr Pepper.

"I wanted to mention something, Dave." Val leaned back in his easy chair. He smiled an easy smile.

"Yes?"

"I found the Sucrets box among some things in your bathroom just now. I dropped the pill in your Dr Pepper, while you were fetching the board. You're about to forget everything. So you had better go ahead and tell me the names of those children so that at least one witness in the world remains: me. I will be the bearer of your secret."

"You . . . you . . . I knew I could never trust you. . . ."

"Better hurry."

"You're a bad person, Val."

"I'm not, really. The names."

Dave sighed. He put his head in his hands.

"No. I'm not telling."

"Might as well. Just their names. How could I possibly do anything with just names? Just names, Dave?"

Dave groaned. He squeezed his head.

"Pauline. And Chance. They're brother and sister. That's all I know. Don't you dare do anything, Val. I don't feel well."

 14

Dave Green put his head between his knees for a moment. Then he sat up straight.

"Remember?" said Val.

"Remember what?"

"Saint Philomene's Infirmary?"

"What?"

"Never mind. You take the white pieces. I'll spot you a queen's knight."

CHAPTER 3

Back in late June, when Chance had been home from Saint Philomene's for a few days, after he finally felt like his cuts had healed, his bruises grown less angry, his bumps diminished, he ventured down the street to Ladystark's Five & Dime, where he purchased an eight-and-a-half-by-eleven-inch blank book with a cover depicting the first Superman comic (*Action Comics No. 1*, June 1938, 10 cents) and four Rapidograph pens, carried everything home, and immediately embarked on a graphic and literary record of his journey to Saint Philomene's Infirmary for Magical Creatures. He worked in secret, twelve hours a day, every day, and was finished in two weeks. The great tragedy of the manuscript was that he could show it to no one, not even Mersey or his sister—especially them. They would consider it too dangerous and risky to even exist, and would make him destroy it. Chance could only enjoy *SPIfMC* by himself.

He hid the manuscript under his mattress, and as time went on, took it out less and less. By early August, he had more or less forgotten about it.

One evening, a couple of days before Mersey had made her announcement about Fred not existing on the internet, Chance had been sitting at the dining room table watching trebuchet videos on YouTube on his mother's laptop. Pauline was at Mersey's, and their mother was in Austin teaching yoga. Fred was watching ESPN.

"Whoa!" said Chance, who'd found a video of a counterpoise trebuchet that could toss a Volkswagen Golf two hundred yards. "Fred! Come look at this one!"

Fred wandered over with a grin on his face and leaned over the laptop as Chance hit REPLAY.

"Wow!" he said. "I think you're certainly spending your summer in the right way, lad."

"Yeah."

"What else have you done this summer? You know, before I was around?"

"Oh, not much."

"Yeah, it's been a boring summer for me, too. Golf, tennis, golf, golf."

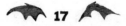 17

Suddenly Chance had an urge. What could it hurt, *really?*

"Wait here," he said, and ran upstairs.

When he came back downstairs, he had the manuscript of *SPIfMC* in one hand.

"I have something to show you, but you have to promise not to tell anyone, including Daisy and Mersey and Pauline."

"Sure, lad, whatever you say."

They sat on the couch.

"Now, the following is something I made up, pure fiction, a story. Just a tale. Okay?"

"Got it."

Chance started at the beginning. The first panel showed a boy digging a hole under a big tree. The text below read:

On an unnaturally hot spring afternoon, the day after the last day of seventh grade, Chance Bee Jeopard, a brown-haired boy of narrow build whose ears stuck out perhaps a bit too far, was digging a hole in the backyard of the small house he shared with his older sister, Pauline, and their mother, Daisy, when plork! Chance's rusty old shovel hit something that was most certainly not dirt.

Chance looked up at Fred. Fred was peering down at the manuscript, an inscrutable look on his face. Chance turned

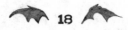

the pages slowly, allowing Fred to read along silently as the characters of Chance, Pauline, and Mersey got involved in the Saint Philomene's Infirmary adventure.

An hour later, when Chance turned the last page and closed the book, he sat quietly and waited for Fred to say something. There was a long moment of silence. Then:

"Quite a story, lad, bravo."

"Thanks, Fred."

Chance was dying to tell him it was not a story, or at least not fiction; it had all happened, for real.

"Ingenious, how the Chance and Pauline characters found their way out through a five-hundred-step staircase and a waterfall, then hopped on a train and rode it straight home."

"Well, it's made up, don't you know."

"Of course."

"Promise you won't tell anyone I showed you?"

"Sure, but why not? They'd be impressed. You wrote a book. You could get it published."

"I—I can't explain it. Just don't tell. Please?"

"Promise."

"Thanks, Fred."

Chance went upstairs, placed the manuscript back under his mattress, changed into his pajamas, and climbed into bed. He thought about how he was no longer alone with his book, how Fred knew about it, too, and this made him happy. Fred even thought it was publishable! Maybe Chance

 19

would rewrite it, change some key elements so no one would be able to find Saint Philomene's, then give it to an important New York publishing house and see what happens. Maybe someday it would appear on the shelves of all the world's libraries.

He heard Pauline in her room next door bustling around—he hadn't heard her come home. Chance was dying to tell her about the manuscript, too, now more than ever. He wanted everyone to know.

CHAPTER 4

After he destroyed Dave Green with the black pieces, then with the white, then with the black again, Val Sleaford took his leave, drove to downtown Lubbock, parked in an alley behind Kaput's Koffee, opened his laptop, accessed Kaput's free Wi-Fi, and began searching *Chance and Pauline*. It wasn't long before he found an obituary for Albert Wuthering Jeopard. The rest was easy. Val took a notebook from his back pocket and wrote his own name down and began scribbling. Then he made a phone call.

"Carver, it's Val."

"Yessir."

"I'll be gone awhile—you won't see me. You'll be in charge. When I get back, we'll be embarking on a new project, maybe a big one. You hear?"

"All right. Where you going?"

"The hottest place in Texas."

Val hung up. He watched a few videos on YouTube, Vimeo. Chance Jeopard after he rescued a puppy, Pauline Jeopard after she discovered some dinosaur footprints, Daisy Jeopard teaching a yoga class. He found a schedule of classes Daisy was teaching at a yoga retreat in Northampton, Massachusetts, early next month. In three minutes he was signed up; in six minutes he had a round-trip ticket from Austin to Boston.

Now he just needed a place to live near the town of Starling. The internet was perfect for apartment hunting; Val found a nice, furnished two-bedroom in the neighboring town of McCandless, and the landlord accepted PayPal for the rent and security deposit.

Then Val sent an e-mail to a very special person.

Dodds:

I need a Social Security number, US passport, and a Texas driver's license in the name of Neville F. Antaso, and bank accounts at Chase set up in the same name, checks and a debit card to be sent to 1405 Warburton Lane,

McCandless, Texas 78705. Photo and signature attached. $50,000 cash will be delivered to the usual drop-off location.

Val

And Valentine Sleaford drove back to his house to pack.

CHAPTER 5

Pauline, Chance, and Mersey sat on the carpet in Pauline's room with a laptop and scratch pads and tried to figure out anagrams of Neville Fred Antaso. A big bowl of Funyuns sat on the floor between them.

"Atlas Lenin Federov?" said Chance, digging into the world's most perfect oniony snack.

"No, he doesn't strike me as Russian," said Mersey. "Besides, no hits in Google."

"Dave Orleans Fintle?" said Pauline.

"Stretching it."

"Allen Stefano Vider?" said Chance. He was having trouble holding his pencil from all the Funyuns grease.

"Good, but no hits," said Mersey.

"Steven Florida Lane?" said Pauline.

"That sounds like an address," said Mersey.

"Well excuse me. Chance, aren't you getting more Funyuns than everyone else?"

Chance could not answer because his mouth was full.

"Dillon Ravenfeaste?" said Pauline.

"Hmm. No."

"Al Vernon Eastfield?" said Chance.

"At least that sounds like a real name," said Mersey. "But no hits."

"I think," said Pauline, rolling onto her back and staring at the ceiling of her room, which was filled with a magnificent orrery, "that we might be going about this the wrong way."

"How so?" said Mersey.

"We should be thinking about this from Fred's perspective. If he is, in fact, using a fake name, then why? What could he be after?"

"What if," said Mersey, lying on her back next to Pauline, head to toe, "he somehow knows about . . . you guys? Your adventures? And wants to get into Saint Philomene's?"

"How could he possibly know?" said Chance, feeling, all of a sudden, very, very bad.

"Two words," said Pauline. "Dave Green."

"But why the charade?"

"If it was in fact Dave Green, we have no idea what he could have told him."

"Okay," said Chance, feeling a little sick to his stomach. "If Fred is really Dave Green's friend, then what is Fred? What interest could he have in Saint Philomene's?"

"He could be a biologist," said Mersey, beginning to thumb-wrestle with her friend.

"A doctor," said Pauline, thumb-wrestling back.

"Those don't sound likely," said Chance. "Why change your name?"

"Something where money is at stake," said Pauline, sitting up now to get a better angle on Mersey.

"A miner?" said Chance.

"Yes!" said Mersey, losing the thumb match and moving over to her laptop. "Googling Texas mining magnates now. Let's see: R. Don Gnusson III. Boyd Unger. Gareth Oym Toynbee. Hart Fasic Meath. Cando Yount. Valentine Sleaford. Campbell Floatus. Groudge—"

"Wait!" Chance said. "What was that one, Valentine . . ."

"Sleaford," said Pauline.

"Scrambling . . . stand by . . ."

Mersey and Pauline watched as Chance crossed out letters on his scratch pad.

"A perfect anagram for Neville Fred Antaso!"

"Well done, Chance. So who in the world is Valentine Sleaford?"

"According to Wikipedia," said Mersey, "he's from Lubbock, and is the leading miner in Texas. All kinds of mining—open pit, strip, long wall, fracking—you name it, he does it."

"Do you think . . . ," said Chance, feeling nauseated.

"I think he wants to find out where Donbaloh is so he can break into it," said Mersey. "Maybe he thinks there's gold there. Heck, maybe there *is*."

"And he's infiltrated our family to find out how to get there," said Pauline, stunned. "I sure haven't told him anything. And no way Chance would say anything. Right, Chance?"

Chance swallowed and said nothing.

"He must just be biding his time," said Mersey, "hoping to corner one of you Jeopards, maybe bribe you with arrowheads or trebuchet bits."

"I can't believe we have an impostor in the house," said Pauline.

"I have to go home, guys," said Mersey, gathering up her laptop. "There is much work to be done tomorrow. Until then, try to act normal. And get some rest."

Chance closed his scratch pad and went to his room. Pauline lay in bed and read about different methods of mining for a while, then turned out the lights.

She felt strange. There was a hollow, ragged, shattered sensation between her lungs that took twenty minutes to identify as heartbreak. Fred had deceived her, her mother,

her brother, Mersey, everyone. A new feeling soon took over, one more familiar, and it was anger. She wished he was still here. She would march downstairs and tell him a thing or two, but he usually went home to his apartment in McCandless after dinner. She didn't have an e-mail for him, but she did know his address, so she wrote him an old-fashioned letter.

Fred (or should I say Valentine),
We know what you're up to, and you won't get away with it. Your lies and deception have come to an end. You can't hurt anyone else. Go back to Lubbock, and stay there.

Sincerely,
Pauline and Chance Jeopard

She put it in an envelope and stamped, sealed, and addressed it. She walked, barefoot—the pavement was still burning hot—down to the mailbox at the street and put up the flag. She looked back up at her house. Her brother's bedroom light was on.

Chance lay in bed, paralyzed. Had Fred—Valentine—been able to tell exactly where Saint Philomene's was from his book? The waterfall near the railroad tracks on the edge of

 28

Big Bend National Park? Gah! He climbed out of bed, lifted up his mattress, reached for his manuscript—and froze.

It was not in its usual position. That is, front cover up, spine out, directly beneath his pillow. This time it was face-down, fore edge out, in the middle of the mattress.

Someone had been looking at it. Chance turned to the salient pages, where, from the text, the location of Saint Philomene's and Donbaloh could be determined.

Had Valentine taken pictures of the pages?

Of course he had.

Chance had to come clean. He had to tell Pauline and Mersey.

He would do it in the morning.

He climbed into bed. Wide-eyed, he stared at the ceiling.

What had he done? What had he done!

Right now Valentine Sleaford might be marshaling his mining equipment over Donbaloh. How long would it take to dig? How long to break through the stone sky of the underground realm?

There was no time to lose. He jumped out of bed and ran to his sister's room and tapped urgently, quietly on the door.

"Pauline! It's me! Open up! It's important!"

Chance felt a tap on his shoulder and stifled a shriek. He turned around to behold his sister.

"What are you doing in the hallway!"

"I had to mail a letter. What are *you* doing in the hallway?"

"I have a confession to make. You're not going to like it."

"Come to my room."

Chance sat at his sister's desk.

"What have you got behind your back?" she said.

Chance handed her the manuscript. Pauline started at the beginning, her mouth opening wider and wider as she read. She flipped to the end, snapped it shut.

"Chance, this is beautiful, but you're not going to tell me that someone has seen this."

Chance sighed.

"Fred. Valentine. I showed it to him. In a weak moment, a few days ago. And sometime over the last couple of days I think he scanned it or otherwise photographed it, without my knowledge or consent. He now knows where Saint Philomene's and Donbaloh are, roughly."

Pauline regarded her brother. It was not a look of contempt, hatred, loathing, anger, or disgust. It was one of compassion. Chance had never loved his sister more than he did in this moment.

"Okay. Okay. What to do? What to do? We have to warn them! Yryssy Ayopy, in Saint Philomene's. Do you still play chess with her? Can you get a message to her?"

"Not anymore. She hasn't been signed on to ChessKnight .com in ages."

Pauline dialed Mersey's number.

"We have a situation. Can you come back over? I'll drop the fire escape ladder out my window."

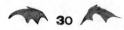

In minutes Mersey was climbing through Pauline's window, looking none too pleased.

"What's going on?" she said.

Pauline explained. Chance shrank so that he became one with the carpet. Mersey thumbed through the manuscript.

"Gorgeous," she said. "You should have shown us, Chance. We wouldn't have been mad."

"I'm sorry I showed Valentine. I thought it was harmless."

"We have two obstacles," said Mersey, all business. "One, we have to stop Valentine, and two, we have to warn Donbaloh. If we can accomplish one, then we don't have to worry about two, but I think accomplishing one is unlikely, so we should concentrate on two. How do we do that?"

"We could get in the same way we got out," said Chance. "Take the train out to the waterfall, descend the five-hundred-step staircase, ride the draisine along the tracks till we get to Saint Philomene's—"

"There are too many risks," said Pauline. "Remember the broken rope bridge? The chasm? The hole we dropped from?"

"Well, what about digging up the mail pipe again?" said Chance.

"That would take forever, and you'd get caught this time for sure," said Mersey.

"I'm out of ideas," said Chance, who chose that moment to lie down flat on the floor.

"Who do you know that knows how to get into Saint Philomene's?"

"Dave Green!" said Chance and Pauline together.

There were sixteen David Greens in the Lubbock directory but only one Dave Green, so Pauline called that one, put it on speakerphone.

"Mr. Green?" said Pauline, trying to sound like her mother, adult and low and responsible.

"It's late, who is this?"

"Pauline Jeopard, I was in Saint Philomene's with you."

"Wha?"

"This is Valentine Sleaford's friend?"

"Yes, I—"

"Please don't pretend you don't remember."

Pauline felt very confident channeling Daisy Jeopard.

"Remember what?"

"I need to know how to get into Saint Philomene's."

"I don't know what you're talking about."

"Yes you do, sir."

"I'm hanging up now. Good-bye."

Pauline found herself listening to the dual pitch of a dial tone. Daisy Jeopard wouldn't have let it get that far.

"Well, maybe he really doesn't remember," said Chance. "It would make sense that Saint Philomene's would be sure he didn't recall being there."

"Yeah, true," said Mersey. "Anybody else?"

"Mersey," said Chance. "Got your laptop?"

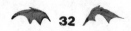

"Yeah," she said, opening a browser window and giving Chance an expectant look. "Shoot."

"Google *Fallor Medoby Dox*. That's F-A-L-L-O-R M-E-D-O-B-Y D-O-X. That was the name on the return address on the envelope I snatched out of the mail pipe in June. It was an Oppabof address. A terrestrial address. A weird one, Pipe something something, Slice something something, but maybe he has a more conventional address, too."

"Nothing," said Mersey. "Trying variants."

Pauline and Chance watched over Mersey's shoulder as her fingers flew over the keyboard.

"Wait, y'all—'Dox, Fal. Med.' An address in Switzerland. What do you think?"

"I think it's him," said Pauline.

"Me too."

"So here's the plan," said Chance. "We use Mersey's dad's FedEx account and send him an international overnight parcel with my manuscript, a letter, and a return box and label."

"Can I stay over?" said Mersey. "I left a note at my house saying I was staying here tonight."

"Sure," said Pauline, who dragged a sleeping bag out from under her bed.

"Thanks!"

Chance stood there, looking rather dazed.

"Chance," said Pauline.

"Yes?"

"Begone!"

CHAPTER 6

Fallor Medoby Dox, one of the few Pacifica Gozo left in the world, and one of only two living in Oppabof (the other, Kirie Daw Gavania, resided in Bucharest and still had *both* his wings), persisted in modest contentment in a small but charmingly appointed flat in the center of Gstaad, Switzerland, waiting each day for the postman to deliver the mail. Fallor was an inveterate collector of books that featured humans or humanoids that could fly or had wings, like himself—though, having only one wing remaining (Fallor lost his right to Klirch-Octia's Distress; the good physicians at Saint Philomene's saved his left), he couldn't even fly around his own living room if he chose.

Among the jewels of his collection was a 1751 first edition of Robert Paltock's *The Life and Adventures of Peter Wilkins*, in which a Cornish man finds himself a castaway in the fantastic land of Normnbdsgrsutt, where men and women can fly. Fallor's copy was bound in citron morocco by the famed British binder Roger Payne in 1780. Fallor also had an inscribed 1984 first edition of Angela Carter's *Nights at the Circus*, about a woman named Fevvers who was born with wings. Also on his shelves was an eight-hundred-year-old manuscript of the Saddharmapuṇḍarīka Sūtra, which features Kinnaris, or women with the wings of swans that inhabit the legendary forest of Himavanta. Many hundreds of other treasures lined his dozens of mahogany bookshelves.

Today Fallor was waiting for a very special book: the editio princeps of the works of Ovid, printed in Rome by Conradus Sweynheym and Arnoldus Pannartz in 1471, which included the first printed account of the legend of Icarus, son of Daedalus, who flew too close to the sun, which melted his waxen wings. Fallor bought the book for a small fortune at the German auction house Reiss & Sohn. He was expecting it to be delivered today.

Fallor paced around his apartment, waiting for the door-bell to ring, drinking a cup of Lapsang souchong and flexing

his eight-foot wing, which he usually kept tightly folded up under a woolen greatcoat, hidden from the world. When it was secreted away, Fallor looked like any old Swiss grandfather, keen about books and tea and the songbirds that frequented the feeders hanging from the boughs of the aspens outside his windowsill.

Uzzzzzz!

"Finally!" said Fallor to himself. He set his cup of tea down and strode to the door.

"Good day, Dr. Dox," said Urszula, the FedEx delivery-woman. "Overnight parcel for you."

"Thank you, my dear, thank you," said Fallor, signing the FedEx thingie. He closed the door and walked over to his dining table.

"Hmm, feels light," he said to himself. He knew the Ovid was a good-sized folio in two parts bound in alum-tawed pigskin over wooden boards and would have some heft. He looked at the return address on the box.

"Texas? This is not my Ovid."

He opened the parcel. Out tumbled a Superman comic book, a letter, and a return box with a label affixed.

The letter read:

Dear Mr. Medoby Dox,
My name is Chance Jeopard. I am a human.
Donbaloh and Saint Philomene's Infirmary are once again in grave danger. A mining company plans to

dig a hole to the realm. I must get inside to warn them, but I do not know how. Can you help me? My sister and I once helped save the Infirmary—our story is told in the enclosed book. Please read it immediately and write back. I would be grateful if you would return the book. Please use the enclosed box and label, which guarantees international overnight delivery at my expense. Discretion and speed are of the utmost importance.

Sincerely,
Chance Jeopard
Starling, Texas

Fallor, feeling suddenly faint, staggered back and fell into a large, overstuffed leather chair in a corner, Chance's letter and manuscript in one hand. He sat still for a long while, taking deep breaths, considering the implications of the missive. Humans in Donbaloh. He had heard about Dave Green. He had heard about the Jeopard siblings, their ingenuity and heroism. Fallor was shocked that Donbaloh could be under threat again so soon. A miner. The mineral wealth in Donbaloh was staggering, trillions of dollars' worth.

He began reading.

Fallor had read many manuscripts. He was impressed by the attention to detail, the careful descriptions. As it

progressed, the illustrations became bolder and were fired off with broader strokes, the text brighter and shot through with grander verbs; by the end it was almost an abstraction. . . .

When he looked up, it was dark outside, and the streetlights shone in the windows, illuminating the books on the shelves. Fallor was exhausted; he felt wetness on his cheeks and dabbed at them with the sleeves of his greatcoat. He sat still, the manuscript in his lap, and thought of Saint Philomene's, where his life was saved, where millions of lives had been saved: Saint Philomene's, and its greater environs, Donbaloh, now in some unnamed peril.

Fallor stood, walked over to one of his many bookcases, removed a huge volume whose spine was titled *Directory of Accesses and Termini*, then sat at his antique escritoire and opened the work to *USA; Texas; Starling*. There was one access to Donbaloh in Starling, through the laundry room of an old dentist's office. There was an asterisk next to it.

*Sealed, 1954.

Curses!

Fallor took an old atlas off the shelf and opened it to Texas. He found Starling. He looked at the surrounding towns. Wanfield, McCandless, Opi, Reusch, Diebenbrock, Flynn. He checked each in *DAT*; only one, Reusch, had an access to Donbaloh. Fallor read the entry, and his heart sank. He took out a sheet of paper and, with an old Mont Blanc fountain pen, began to write.

When he was finished, Fallor folded the letter, placed it in the return box along with Chance's manuscript, and sealed it up. He donned his *gletscherhut*, secured his greatcoat about his shoulders, and made his way out into the world. On the corner of Alpinastrasse and Kirchweg, three blocks away, he deposited the parcel in a lonesome FedEx box.

He looked around. Towering, snow-covered mountains rose in nearly every direction, and one could ski any day of the year. Fallor did not ski. Fallor, at one time, flew over mountains, and did not need to ski.

He walked back to his apartment. The daily mail had not yet arrived.

CHAPTER 7

Neville Fred Antaso was gone. Chance and Pauline watched their mother carefully for signs of heartbreak and despair, but she exhibited none. They found out later Fred had left her a note saying he'd moved to Tibet on business and couldn't be reached. He'd be gone indefinitely.

The earliest they could expect to hear from Fallor Medoby Dox, if it was in fact him they'd sent the parcel to, was two days after they'd first posted it. They mailed it on a Wednesday. When Friday came around, Pauline, Mersey, and Chance would watch from the big picture window in the living room for the white, orange, and blue FedEx van to come rolling down the street.

Meanwhile, the friends were doing everything they could to stop Valentine Sleaford from starting his mining project.

"It looks like most of the property on the edge of Big Bend around the town of Rincón Oscuro is owned by a woman named Frieda Bull Radegast," said Mersey, studying a land survey on her laptop. "It's about six thousand two hundred fifty acres called the Lazy Yucca Ranch, and is right over Donbaloh."

"Valentine would have to have permission from her to mine on her property," said Chance.

"Let's call her," said Pauline.

Mersey found a number, dialed, and handed the phone to Pauline, who again channeled Daisy Jeopard.

"Hello?" said a woman's voice, deep and resonant.

"May I speak with Miss Frieda Radegast?"

"You already are. What's this about?"

"My name is Pauline Jeopard. I have reason to believe a man named Valentine Sleaford is going to try to contact you—"

"He already has. Fact he's sitting out on my porch drinking my limeade. What you got to tell me 'bout him?"

"He wants to mine on your property, but it will do irreparable damage to the Earth. I beg you not to let him."

41

"How old're you?"

"He—broke my mother's heart."

Pauline winced. *Where did that come from?*

"I see."

"He's a bad man."

This was not going well, not according to plan.

"He's offering me a whole lotta money."

"Please don't let him."

"I'm afraid I'm gonna tell him yes, young lady. I need the money. I'm sorry about your mother."

Pauline sat down on the floor and tried not to sigh.

"Will you not tell him I called?"

"All right."

"And one more thi—"

But Frieda Bull Radegast had hung up.

"Well, we've got our work cut out for us now," said Chance with a sigh.

"How can we stop a miner from mining?" said Pauline.

"I have some ideas," said Mersey, and the look in her eye said that she really, truly did.

The next day was Friday. They watched the street through the big picture window. They saw a UPS truck, the mailman, even a DHL delivery van, but no FedEx.

"I don't think that was him we sent the parcel to," said Chance.

"Me neither," said Pauline.

"You guys are such wet blankets," said Mersey. "I'm confident we sent it to the right guy."

The afternoon dragged on.

And then, at 6:14 p.m., a white, orange, and blue van stopped right at their house.

They ran to the door.

Chance signed for the parcel, because it was addressed to him. He took it to the dining room, tore the box open, and spilled the contents out onto the table.

"My book! And a letter!"

Chance, his hands trembling, unfolded the crisp, hand-made paper.

Dear Chance,
A most extraordinary and moving document and record, your manuscript, and I wonder how you knew to send it to me? I wish I was acquainted with someone who could be an emissary for you; indeed I wish I could go myself, but I am far too infirm to travel, so it seems that it must be you. I had hoped the road to Donbaloh would be a smooth one, but it seems that it is not: You must go to the Ulphine Caverns near the neighboring town of Reusch, and bring with you waterproof flashlights, an inflatable raft (collapsed), an inflator, an oar, and life vests, one for you and each of your companion travelers.

43

There is no need for disguises, as humans have been decriminalized. Enter the main cavern, follow the central artery 1150 yards until a small, clear pool is reached. Get into the pool, take a deep breath, swim 107 feet underwater, north-northwest through a narrow tunnel in the rock, until you surface in swiftly running water. This is the Yalphala River. Climb onto the bank, inflate the boat, don the life vests, and launch. Beware of violent rapids. In about six hours expect to arrive in Donbaloh, a vast cavern whose stone sky rises twelve miles above you. The first thing you will see will be the entrance to the Donbaloh Public Library. Enter the library and ask how to obtain an emergency audience with Tylotch Plariant, the prefect of Donbaloh. I warn you, Plariant is a bit eccentric. This is the best I can advise you.

Bel chasse,

Fallor M. Dox

"Whoa!" said Chance, folding the letter up and holding it to his chest. "One hundred seven feet underwater! I can do that!"

"I'm pretty sure I can," said Pauline, looking unsure. She took the letter from her brother and began reading it again.

"I can't," said Mersey, crestfallen. She had wanted to go

this time. "You guys know I can't even hold my breath for ten seconds without getting dizzy and panicky."

The siblings nodded solemnly. They knew. "Looks like I'm your Oppabof contact again," Mersey continued. "But listen, Killiam has an inflatable raft, plus he can take you two to the Ulphine Caverns in his pickup."

"What are you kids plotting?" said Daisy, surprising everyone. She had just emerged from her yoga room. "What's that you've got there?"

"Just a graphic novel that came from Switzerland," said Chance, who was no good at lying but occasionally excellent at deception. He handed it to his mother. She flipped through it without apparent interest, handed it back, and picked up the box. "Gstaad! A beautiful place, surrounded by mountains. I hope you didn't pay too much shipping, young man. Pauline, what have you got behind your back?"

Mersey, who was standing behind Pauline, surreptitiously snatched the letter away from Pauline. Pauline showed her empty hands to her mother.

"My children are so odd. But I love them so. And you too, Mersey. What can I make y'all to eat?"

"Mac and cheese?" said Chance.

"You got it."

After dinner Mersey went home to scheme on preventing Valentine Sleaford from mining Frieda Radegast's property, and Chance took his sister aside.

"Pauline, we have to go as soon as possible."

"I know. Chance, I'm worried I won't be able to hold my breath that long."

"That's why we're going to the Ernie tonight after Mom goes to sleep."

"Ernie! Swimming!"

The E. K. Earnest Community Pool was fifteen blocks away and open till midnight.

Even after ten at night it was still ninety-five degrees in the town of Starling, the sidewalk burning under their feet. Bugs wheeled around the streetlights, and bats wheeled around after the bugs. The siblings were the only people out; no cars drove down the deserted streets, and only a semi's air brakes could be heard on the freeway a quarter mile away. On the way, Chance and Pauline discussed everything they'd need for the journey.

"The fulgurite fragments for sure," said Pauline, walking along the curb, her arms out for balance. "Our only contact with Mersey, and possibly each other, if we get separated."

Some varieties of fulgurite, the mineral produced when lightning strikes certain types of soil, have communicative properties—fragments of the same fulgurite branch allow the bearers to communicate telepathically. Pauline, Mersey, and Chance happened to have fragments of this type of fulgurite.

"I think sharp pocketknives," offered Chance.

"I'll bring my five-dollar gold piece," said Pauline, losing her balance, falling off the curb into the street, and immediately jumping back up again.

"If the rapids on the Yalphala River are that bad, maybe we'll need some rope to secure us to the raft."

"What about underwater flashlights?"

"Maybe we can get those at Academy, or somewhere else that sells camping supplies," said Chance.

"Speaking of getting," said Pauline, "how much money do we have, altogether? I have about thirty-nine bucks."

"I have about eight," said Chance. The pool was less than a block away. It always excited him to come here. Chance was a great swimmer.

"I don't know if that'll be enough for everything."

They walked up to the fence surrounding the pool.

"Who's that?"

A single solitary person was in the water, methodically swimming laps at the east edge of the hundred-foot pool.

"I think that's Mrs. Applebaker!"

Mrs. Applebaker, their neighbor, the woman who'd loaned Chance the shovel he'd used to dig the hole in which he'd discovered the mail pipe that led to Saint Philomene's in June.

She had a very bright LED flashlight strapped to her forehead. Pauline and Chance watched her for a while, then stripped down to their suits and jumped in the water at the shallow end.

"Hi, Mrs. Applebaker!"

"Well hi, Jeopards!" She switched off her light and waded over. "What brings you out here?"

"Practicing underwater swimming."

"Ah," she said. "A worthy skill indeed."

"Where'd you get that neat flashlight headgear?"

"On the World Wide Interwebs. Got a bunch at home. Want a couple?"

Chance and Pauline looked at each other and grinned.

"Can we? We'll bring 'em back."

"We'll all ride home together and you can come in for a minute and I'll set you up. I'm staying till closing, that okay?"

"Yeah! Thanks!"

"You bet."

Mrs. Applebaker swam off to finish her laps.

"Okay, Pauline, all you have to do is swim one length plus seven feet. Now, in the cavern, you're probably not going to get to push off of a wall, so you can't do that here, either. Just start swimming from a standing position. Take a few deep breaths, then one really deep breath, and go. Swim toward that light at the other end—see? You can do it!"

Pauline looked down at the wavering reflections in the water, at her hands, feet. She closed her eyes, took three breaths, then a deep breath, and dove under the water. She swam as hard as she could toward the light affixed to the wall at the far end. It seemed like it wasn't getting any closer. Her lungs burned; they felt like they would burst. She came up for air about twenty feet from the end of the pool, gasping, choking, flailing.

"Good!" shouted Chance. "Great first try! Come on back."

Pauline swam back to her brother. She felt like crying, but she held it back.

"That was terrible," she said.

"Not at all, that was amazing," he said, patting his sister on the back. "We're going to wait a few minutes, and this time, I want you to take a deeper breath, swim without resting, and keep your head down. Okay?"

"'Kay."

This time Pauline made it ten feet closer to the wall. The next time she made it all the way. But after four more tries she couldn't quite make 107 feet.

A lifeguard came out of nowhere and announced that the E. K. Earnest Community Pool was closed.

Pauline felt a kind of despair coming on. There was no way she was going to let her brother go by himself. But she really didn't want to die in an underwater tunnel, either.

"A bathing cap will help," whispered Chance in the back seat of Mrs. Applebaker's car. "Tame all that crazy red hair that's slowing you down. All you have to do is practice holding your breath as much as you can."

Mrs. Applebaker gave them each an underwater headlamp. They thanked her and snuck back into their own house.

CHAPTER 8

Early the next morning Pauline jumped on her brother's bed to wake him up.

"Chance, rise and shine!"

"Stop!"

Chance was exhausted. So much had happened. So much to come. But the next part was going to be the hardest. Chance had absolutely no desire to lie to his mother, or anyone, but it would have to be done.

"I have an idea about how to buy us a few days," said Pauline, as Chance brushed his teeth. "When you're done, come downstairs."

Chance rinsed, dressed, combed his hair, and reluctantly went downstairs. Without a word, his sister picked up the phone and dialed.

"Hello, Jones here."

"Uncle Jones? Hi, it's Pauline. Can Chance and I come and stay with you in Austin for a few days?"

"Why surely," said Uncle Jones, who was their father Albert's brother and loved his niece and nephew. "When?"

"Today?"

"Why, what's the hurry?"

"We miss you."

Pauline loved her uncle, and hated the deception, but lives were at stake.

"Well, aren't you kind. Want me to come fetch you?"

"No thank you, we'll take Greyhound, and call you when we get there."

"Okeydoke. Bye for now."

"Mom!" shouted Pauline at the house at large. "Uncle Jones invited me and Chance to Austin for a few days can we go pleeeeeeeeeease!"

"Okay, but you'll have to bus it!" came Daisy's voice from deep within the house.

Pauline called Uncle Jones back.

"Looks like we can't come after all. Mom has stuff for us to do here."

"Oh dang. Want me to talk to her?"

"No, that's okay, we'll try to come next week, if that works?"

"Surely."

"Love you," said Pauline.

"Love you back," said Uncle Jones.

"Well," said Pauline, clicking off. "That's taken care of. Mom thinks we'll be at Uncle Jones's, and Uncle Jones thinks we'll be here. No one will know we'll be in Donbaloh."

"I hate all the lying," said Chance. "I really don't like it."

"Me too, but it can't be helped."

Daisy came down the stairs.

"What time do you want me to take you to the bus?" she said, opening the refrigerator and finding a container of peach yogurt.

"Oh, Killiam is going to take us," said Pauline. "Around noon."

Chance winced. More lies! He tried to remember that it was all for a good cause.

"I don't want you to be any trouble to your uncle. He has a weak heart, and he's too generous."

"Don't worry."

Killiam Ng and Mersey Marsh showed up in Killiam's battered old green Ford F-150 at 11:40 a.m. Mersey and Pauline and Chance climbed in the back, and they drove to the outskirts of the town of Reusch, down an old dirt road to

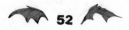

the entrance of a cavern overgrown with bamboo. Killiam stayed in the truck while the friends sorted everything out.

"We'll stay in touch by fulgurite," said Mersey, handing out necklaces of jute threaded with a hollow fragment of fulgurite. They were slippery in Mersey's hands; she had gotten somewhat overheated in the back of the truck and was feeling kind of sticky in all her black clothes and makeup.

"We should have asked FMD how to get *out*, too," said Chance, putting his necklace on over his head. "That was an error."

"We'll ask Tylotch Plariant," said Pauline, putting on her necklace, anxious to get on with things. She was very nervous about the water tunnel and wanted to get it over with.

"I hate long good-byes," said Mersey, her necklace already about her neck. She hugged her two friends and shooed them along on their adventure.

Pauline and Chance, each with a small backpack of equipment, Chance hauling the inflatable raft and battery-operated inflator, parted the bamboo and entered the cavern.

They immediately needed their headlamps and so put them on. The cavern, about twenty feet across and eight feet high, was humid and cool. It seemed there was a different species of gigantic spider in every cranny.

"This is the creepiest place I have ever seen," said Chance.

The footing was slick. It sloped ever-so-gently downward.

The cave gradually enlarged, so that when they reached the end, it was some sixty feet by thirty feet. The pool, a pellucid blue that seemed illuminated from within, could have been ten feet deep or ten thousand.

Chance stripped to his suit, placed his clothes in a waterproof bag, and climbed in the water. He dove down, came back up after a minute.

"I found the tunnel."

"Yeah?"

"It's very narrow, Pauline. It's not going to be easy to swim."

"I can do it."

"Okay. I'm going first; I'll bring all the equipment. You follow about two minutes after me."

Chance loaded his backpack, the inflatable raft, and the inflator in its waterproof pouch, then took a deep breath before diving down to the tunnel. He swam as hard and fast as he could. His hands kept bumping against the rock walls, and once he bumped his head against the low rock ceiling, but he kept going. It seemed like it went on forever, far longer than 107 feet, and he thought he would run out of breath, but eventually he came out the other end, surfacing in a river. He swam to a soft riverbank, tried to catch his breath. He realized his sister was now in the tunnel. She would not make it. He took a deep, deep breath, dove back in the water, and swam again to the tunnel.

He encountered Pauline about three quarters of the way

along, panic in her eyes. He blew air into her lungs through her nose, then hugged the rock, to get out of her way. She swam past him, down the tunnel. Chance nearly got stuck turning around in the cramped space but managed to compress himself into a tight ball and reverse direction. Both Pauline and Chance eventually emerged in the river, gulping air, crying, laughing, incredulous that they had made it alive.

"That was more than one hundred seven feet!" shouted Chance, swimming for the muddy riverbank.

"Sure was, more like one hundred seventy!" yelled Pauline, swimming after her brother, her voice echoing in the eerie chamber.

"Let's blow up this baby and get going," said Chance. "There's no time to lose."

The raft inflated without a hitch. The siblings donned their life jackets. They threaded a rope through the oarlocks to hold on to during the rapids.

"Okay, let's go."

They launched the raft.

For the first hour they floated rapidly but serenely. The river stretched about sixty feet across, the rocky ceiling and arch spiny with stalactites forty feet above. Everything was mysteriously illuminated with a greenish-orange light, like a billiard hall in a van Gogh painting.

Occasionally fish would jump. One landed in the raft. It had the body of an ordinary carp but the face of a tiny

human skull. Instead of fins, it was equipped with six skinny legs, each of which terminated in a kind of many-fingered hand.

"Let me out! Let me out!" it cried, and used its legs to scurry out of the raft and back into the water, leaving a trail of luminous slime.

"We're back," said Chance.

The pace of the Yalphala River slowly accelerated, and a rapid appeared here and there. The banks grew steep, almost vertical—the river must have been very deep. They could not see more than a hundred yards in front of them, though there was a sense that they were descending fairly rapidly. Chance kept the raft in the middle of the river by using the oar as a rudder.

Suddenly the light was gone, and they were in complete darkness.

"Where are the headlamps?"

"I don't know!" shouted Pauline. "Hold on to the rope!"

They picked up speed, slowed briefly, spun 180 degrees, as if in a vortex, then were sucked into a steep flume that curved and rolled and hairpinned, with the black water of the Yalphala rushing all around them as they hung on for dear life and struggled to keep from capsizing. They were each hoping and praying that at the end of the flume was not a hundred-foot or, heaven forbid, a thousand-foot waterfall, but as Providence would have it, that is exactly what was there: The raft with the Jeopards on it, tightly gripping

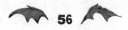

the nylon rope, was suddenly flung, Frisbee-like, into space over a spill of midnight water that dropped off into nothing, Pauline and Chance tumbling in free fall alongside the wall of water, getting ever closer, till finally merging with it, then crashing into a spray of mist hundreds of feet below.

The greenish-orange light had returned to illuminate the underground world. Pauline and Chance were still holding on to the raft by the rope, floating in the calmer water some distance from the base of the waterfall. The Yalphala continued on.

They picked up speed again, floating on uniformly for more than an hour, until they suddenly slowed down and entered a narrow channel that appeared man-made, or, more properly, creature-made. Then:

On the right bank they came upon a pair of hundred-foot metal statues of griffon-like creatures guarding a broad staircase that led to a building hewn out of solid rock. As they floated by, they read the legend on the lowermost frieze: DONBALOH PUBLIC LIBRARY.

"That's the place, Pauline! This is our stop!"

Chance guided the raft to the bank, and they disembarked. He deflated the raft, rolled it up, and hid it near a piling, along with the inflator.

"Let's each hide behind a griffon to change out of our suits back into dry clothes," said Chance.

"I'll take the left one," said Pauline, digging through her backpack for the waterproof pouch that held her clothes.

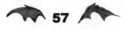

She ducked behind the griffon and ran her hands across its smooth, cool surface. It was made of solid metal. Not silver, which would tarnish—perhaps platinum or palladium. Absolutely priceless. Even if it were nickel or chromium, it would be invaluable. This was what Valentine was after.

Pauline had nearly died twice, just in the last few hours—in the tunnel and in the waterfall. Yet she felt perfectly normal, even happy. What was the matter with her? Did she have a death wish? No, she realized. She was on a mission.

She changed and waited for her brother.

Chance wondered if he should have come by himself. His sister, as tough and resilient and determined and resourceful as she was, might get hurt. He didn't care if *he* got hurt. That had been a close call in the tunnel, and anything could have happened tumbling over that waterfall. He changed into jeans and his favorite Möbius-strip T-shirt, came out from behind the griffon, and signaled to his sister.

"Ready to go?"

"Let's leave these backpacks. Stuff everything we need in our pockets."

"Good idea."

"We should signal Mersey."

Chance thought, *Mersey, are you there?*

I was so worried about you! came Mersey's telepathic reply.

We made it, thought Pauline. *We're in front of the library.*

Be careful.

How's it going in Oppabof?

 58

I've convinced a sympathetic party to sneak onto Frieda Bull Radegast's land and carve fake dinosaur footprints. Hopefully, someone will think they're real, and it will prevent Valentine from getting a permit to mine. Might not work, but there's a chance.

Good thinking.

Signing off.

"Okay, Chance, to the library."

Strangely, there were 107 steps leading up to the entrance of the Donbaloh Public Library. The main revolving door was a huge structure of crystal, gold, and carbon. The Jeopards pushed, and it swung easily on a perfectly balanced central axis. They found themselves in a vast atrium lined floor to ceiling with ancient books of all sizes, each with a small vellum label on the tail of the spine. At left was an information booth, occupied by a creature of a species they had never encountered: a feathered beast, but not a bird, built along the lines of a small bear but standing upright and wearing a vest, trousers, spectacles, and porkpie hat, with a meerschaum pipe, unlit, stuck in the corner of its mouth. The largest book either Chance or Pauline had ever seen lay open before it on the reception desk, which was carved from pink granite.

"If anybody knows where Tylotch Plariant is, it's going to be that guy," said Pauline, gesturing toward the creature. "Let's ask it."

They approached the desk, the edge of which was at forehead level on Chance. He stood on tiptoes.

"Sir—"

"I am not a 'sir,' sir."

"Ma'am—"

"I am not a 'ma'am,' either."

"Oh. Well."

"I am an Yfposton, and you, human, may address me as Esteemed Librarian."

"Esteemed Librarian, I am trying to find Prefect Tylotch Plariant."

The Yfposton peeled the spectacles from its feathery face, placed them in a vest pocket, leaned forward on the desk, and looked hard at Chance.

"The prefect," said the Esteemed Librarian, "is not easily accessible."

"Why?"

"Look," said Pauline, before the Yfposton could answer. "Donbaloh is in danger. We're here to warn Plariant so he can take appropriate action. We need to speak with him."

"Tylotch Plariant is a very busy Ult Thivish."

"Can you direct us?" said Pauline.

"I cannot. The Ult Thivish are a restless, itinerant species, and the prefect could be anywhere in Donbaloh right now."

"Who *can* direct us?" said Chance.

"The Office of the Prefecture won't tell you anything," said the Esteemed Librarian, "and moreover Tylotch Plariant is jealously guarded by his aide-de-camp, Darly de Phanxaire,

a wary and paranoid Femma-Thladrook. One has to get through her to get to him."

"Can you give us any advice at all?"

The Esteemed Librarian studied the siblings, darkly, for a long minute.

"I know who you are, humans. You had a price on your heads until only a couple of months ago—there were wanted posters of you plastered all over Donbaloh, and there are probably some Donbalese out there that don't know that those offers have been rescinded. I know that you acted honorably, in the interest of Saint Philomene's. So I will help you. Listen: My boyfriend lives and works in Saint Philomene's. Go to him. He will take you to a night-club, the Igneo Lounge, on the top floor of the Undercover Federation Building, where his friend Rougi Fatol works as a bouncer."

"How can Rougi help us?"

"Rougi, a type of creature known as a Fylaria-Lit, is Darly de Phanxaire's fiancé. Rougi, as tough as he looks, is a kind, reasonable fellow, and can talk sense into Darly. Go in Saint Phil's southwest entrance, take an express to the 5,999th floor—"

"Wait, the 5,999th?"

"Yes."

"Your boyfriend wouldn't happen to be Rob Nthn, would it?"

"Why yes. How did you know?"

"Well, I hear he has a key to the Commodore Club, and can speak on the PA whenever he wants to. He's very important."

"Yes."

"And I heard he had been dating a vampiress."

Chance tried to keep a straight face. When he and his sister were last in Donbaloh, they had spent their entire visit in a vast hospital, Saint Philomene's Infirmary. At the time, it had been illegal to be a human in the underground realm, so they had worn a variety of disguises. Pauline had masqueraded as a vampiress and been wooed by the creature that was now the Esteemed Librarian's boyfriend, Rod Nthn.

"That's old news, and she was, er, not his type. I'm his one true love."

"You must be very happy."

"Soul mates."

"Do you have a phone?" said Pauline.

"Pay phones are in the basement."

"I don't have any money. I just need to call information and then make a local call; I'll be quick," said Pauline.

"Sorry. Pay phones in the basement."

Pauline summoned her deepest, most resonant and critical voice. She said:

"As I said, Esteemed Librarian, Donbaloh is in danger. *Great* danger. When I finally do meet and speak with Tylotch Plariant, I will remark to him that it was *you* that put at risk millions of lives for want of a few *clahd*, and it will be your

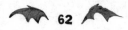

name that will forever be associated with the destruction of Donbaloh. Now are you going to give me your telephone?"

The Esteemed Librarian, looking exasperated, began to root through its purse, a Murakami fake obviously imported from Oppabof. The Esteemed Librarian handed Pauline a coin, a ten-clahd piece—the local version of a dime.

"Downstairs," it said, pointing imperiously at a dark staircase. Pauline and Chance ran.

They found a bank of phones.

"Chance, I think we could use help," said Pauline, dialing a number. "So I've got an idea."

"Directory assistance."

"Um, Saint Philomene's, Braig Toop, please."

"Is this who I think it is?" said the directory assistance creature, with whom Pauline had a checkered past.

"Yeah, sorry."

"Please hold."

"Braig here."

Braig was a Wreau, an endangered creature, and a part-time actor. He had been instrumental in saving Saint Philomene's Infirmary from the threats of Dave Green.

"Braig, Pauline."

"Pau—*Pauline*! What in the world?"

"Chance and I are in Donbaloh. We need your help."

"Oh no, what is it now?"

"Best to explain in person. We're at the public library, main branch. Can you meet us?"

"'Main branch.' I always thought that a bit of a contradiction in terms. How about halfway? The Mifply Currency Exchange Booth at Enchlang Square? Follow the Yalphala River a quarter mile, past Right Bank Community College, the Strangelady Heliport, and the Chochky Diamond Mercantile."

"We're on our way."

As the siblings progressed along the bank of the river, Donbaloh opened up. Buildings sprang up everywhere, some freestanding, others cut into the rock and climbing hundreds, thousands of feet into the air. The ceiling was so high as to be invisible—only a churning umber blackness punctured by the occasional movement of dots of light was in evidence above them. It was (it had to be) the largest cavern in the world. Donbaloh, home of Saint Philomene's Infirmary, and so much more. It was a city, a country, a world.

And it was under siege by yet another madman—a venal, calculating one.

The Mifply Currency Exchange accepted gold bullion. Pauline handed over her five-dollar gold piece. The clerk, a young Thropinese with a stylish center part, assayed her Indian half-eagle coin.

"Can't say I've seen one of these in a while," said the Thropinese, whose crooked smile Pauline found endearing. "How'd you get in?"

"Yalphala."

"That right?"

"Yep."

"Here's one hundred sixteen clahd."

"Is that all?"

"Gold's not worth much down here, I'm sorry to say. We've got an awful lot of it."

"Really?"

"Yeah. About five thousand cubic meters. More than half again all the gold ever mined in history."

"Wow. Is anything valuable down here?"

"Nylon and rub—"

"Pauline! Chance!"

"Braig!"

He looked just the same, a bit like a very tall, furless meerkat. Perhaps he'd lost a pound or two.

"Let's drop into a restaurant and you can tell me what this is all about. The Nosebag Diner is good, right around the corner from here. Good grilled mantle rat sandwiches and welft tea. What say you?"

"Sounds great," said Chance, though the idea of grilled mantle rat turned his stomach a little. Pauline, on the other hand, had an iron gut, a lead palate, and would try anything.

At the Nosebag, Braig ordered for everyone from a short Vyrndeet in a tartan skirt. While they waited for their food, Pauline explained the situation concerning Valentine Sleaford and Donbaloh.

Braig looked thoughtful. He chewed. He sipped tea. Then he said:

"I am astonished and saddened and alarmed. I probably do not need to tell you what would happen if this Valentine were to succeed in puncturing our sky. First of all, our atmosphere has a different nitrogen/oxygen ratio than yours. Humans can tolerate our air, but most Donbalese would not be able to breathe yours. Second, the atmospheric Oppaboffian poisons of methane and ozone are toxic to us. Third, our air pressure is half yours. A sudden increase would sicken the population, and kill many of them."

"How many in Donbaloh?" said Pauline.

"About eight and a half million, plus nearly two million at Saint Philomene's, and another two hundred thousand at the University of Donbaloh ten months of the year. We have a large uncounted transient population as well. So perhaps a peak of eleven million creatures at any given time."

"How thick is the layer of rock between Oppabof and Donbaloh?"

"The ceiling, which is twelve miles above you, is only about four hundred feet thick. Geologically speaking, basically a sheet of onionskin paper. How quickly can a miner poke through that?"

"Just a moment," said Pauline.

Mersey, are you there?

Standing by.

How long would it take for Valentine to dig through four hundred feet of rock? That's how deep Donbaloh is.

Oh my, that's not much, is it? I'll find out.

Any news?

Killiam is bugging me. He wants to know what I'm so involved in lately.

You can't tell him, Mersey.

I know.

"Every so often an oil speculator will drill through to Donbaloh. Since they find no oil, they give up and we patch the hole and that's that."

"We think Valentine believes there's more than just oil down here," said Chance.

"There is. There's everything."

"So we need to speak with Tylotch Plariant immediately. Can you help us?"

Braig took a big bite of mantle rat muffuletta.

"Tylotch Plariant," Braig said eventually, "is jealously guarded . . ."

"Yes, we've been advised of Darly," said Chance. "But we have an idea about her."

"Really."

Braig looked expectant and not a little skeptical. Pauline told him about Rod Nthn and Rougi Fatol.

"Well, let's go see this Rod Nthn," said Braig, standing up and pitching some clahd on the table.

"Even though humans are legal now, we'd best stick to less-traveled roads and thus avoid the Balliope constabulary," said Braig, ducking down a dark alley lined with extravagantly dented garbage cans. "There's not much time to lose, so try to keep up."

Braig hopped and caromed, skipped and ducked, leaped and dodged, racing along the alleyway past piles of trash, strange encampments, gamblers gambling, urchins urching, lost souls crying out for the gods that had abandoned them, all the while in the distance a low din slowly grew in volume, in decibel, in fury as they ran. Ahead, a tall sliver of yellow-crimson came into view at the end of the alleyway, marking the beginning of . . . what?

Braig stopped.

"Forcadel Square," he said, panting. "Something's going on there, ahead, where the alley lets out. It's usually deserted this time of night. We must approach with caution."

Another hundred yards and they were suddenly thrust into Forcadel Square with thousands of other creatures, many holding signs and chanting something that neither Chance nor Pauline could at first discern but which resolved into clarity when an extraordinarily strident Fauxgre joined the chorus:

Ty-lotch Death-watch! Ty-lotch Death-watch!

Pauline yelled at Braig and Chance over the roar of the crowd: "Did you hear that?"

"Yeah!" said Chance. "What's going on?"

"I'll ask," said Braig, who walked up to a Euvyd with an eye patch. Braig remained in conference with her for a while, then ushered Pauline and Chance back into the relative calm of the alley.

"So," said Braig, "it seems that Tylotch Plariant has issued an unpopular edict."

"What?" said Chance.

"A certain tax."

"Well?" said Pauline.

"A left-sock tax."

"What?" said Pauline and Chance together.

"Socks are big business here in Donbaloh. One really can't go barefoot, and one really can't wear shoes without them; the combination of our leather and our swampy atmosphere argues against socklessness."

"But . . . the *left* sock?" said Pauline.

"The prefect's sense of humor," said Braig. "He knows no one will wear just one sock. But that's what's enraging the folks in Forcadel Square right now. They're calling for his head. Plariant is in hiding. *Real* hiding, not just his typical evasive maneuvering. Which is going to make things difficult for us."

"I still say we find Rod Nthn and see if he can connect us with Rougi Fatol," said Chance.

"Agreed," said Braig. "The only way is through that crowd. Hold hands and follow me."

The trio slid into the heaving ruck, which was growing

more and more agitated. Some creatures were putting down their signs and rolling up their shirtsleeves, and others were beating a hasty exit. Then Chance saw a Giant Cpulba bend over and take off his *right* sock. It looked like a huge, dirty gray Christmas stocking made of canvas and felt.

Chance elbowed his sister.

"What's it doing?"

Suddenly a bullhorn sounded at the opposite end of the square.

"Citizens of Donbaloh, you have illegally gathered and must disperse, lest we the constabulary assert our duty to suppress and immure the guilty!"

The Giant Cpulba rolled up his sock—as big as a volleyball—packed it tight, and shot-putted it across the square into the halberd-toting throng of Balliopes, where it was caught, one-handed, by none other than Chet, chief of Saint Philomene's security forces, and Pauline and Chance's great nemesis. Chet brought the sock-ball to his nose, sniffed, and appeared to swoon.

"Chance, did you see that?"

"I saw. What's Chet doing here?"

"We can't let him see us. Braig—"

Then all the creatures in the crowd began taking off their right socks, rolling them up, and firing them at the Balliopes. The crowd pressed in from all sides, and they found themselves carried along by a tide of sock-ball-hurling creatures. The roar of the demonstrators overwhelmed

every effort at communication. Chance held on to Pauline's hand for dear life, but the surge within the sea of creatures was slowly and surely testing the limits of their grasp, and then, just like that, they were separated.

There are perhaps no bodily odors so sharp and pervasive as those produced by the glands of an endocrine system of a creature experiencing the pique of revolt, and certainly no easier way for these odors to propagate than for thousands of socks to be removed at once. Chance found himself verily submerged in the unbreathable corporeal perfumes of scores of unwashed, partially sockless species pressing against him like the atmosphere of Jupiter.

Chance began to feel light-headed.

CHAPTER 9

Chance awoke in blackness. He was prone, covered in some blanket that smelled like corn chowder. His head felt like a gourd poached in kerosene. Something about the hardness of the surface upon which he lay and the disposition of the dark suggested he was on the floor, on a thin throw rug. He listened: The distant sounds of a city could be heard. He tried to move, found it difficult. Ah! His hands were tied behind his back, and he was tethered to a wall. *What the . . . ?*

The crowd. It was all slowly coming back to him. The *odeur*.

How long ago had he fainted? Where were Pauline and Braig? Oh, did his head *hurt*.

The clangor of a key in a lock, the twist of a doorknob, the creak of ancient door hinges, a shaft of light, expanding, then diminishing, and then darkness again at the instant the door slammed shut. Footsteps. A click, a bright light, and Chance looked up, squinting, to behold a vast Harrow-Teaguer, arms filled with grocery bags.

"Well, look who's up."

"Who are you?"

"Who am *I*? Who are *you*?"

"Chance Jeopard. From Oppabof."

"Well, I gathered that second bit. What do you want here? What were you doing at the demonstration?"

"What happened?"

"You passed out; there was a stampede; I saved you."

Chance rolled onto his side and studied the vast creature, the yellow horn with the blue tip protruding from its forehead, the black scales covering its body, its massive, muscular legs, its two-fingered "hands" that could pop a coconut like a cherry tomato.

"I was trying to get to Saint Philomene's Infirmary with my sister. We got separated. I need to find her."

Chance suddenly remembered the fulgurite around his neck. He looked down.

Gone!

Panic seized him. This was apparently not lost on the Harrow-Teaguer.

"What's the matter, Chance Jeopard?"

"Nothing. I have to get to Saint Philomene's."

"Hmm. That's not going to happen."

"What? Why?"

"I just looked you up on the internet here. You're wanted, and worth money: ten thousand clahd."

"You are mistaken, Harrow-Teaguer. Old news. Those wanted signs were rescinded. I'm legal; all humans are legal. Look it up. Perform your due diligence."

"Good try. You're very convincing. But I'm going to go down to the lobby and find me a Balliope and collect my money."

Chance sighed. "I suppose it wouldn't do any good to explain why I'm here, that it's a matter of life and death, that if you turn me over to the Balliopes it may mean the destruction of Donbaloh."

The Harrow-Teaguer began to laugh. "I don't see how."

"Well . . ."

"Silence!"

"There is a human named Valentine Sleaford . . ."

"I do not wish to hear it!"

". . . and he is a very powerful miner in Oppabof . . ."

The Harrow-Teaguer reached into a grocery bag and withdrew an object that looked much like a cross between a baseball and a pincushion, strode over to Chance, pinched

his nose until he opened his mouth, then jammed the object between his teeth.

"Nngluh," said Chance.

"There," said the Harrow-Teaguer, pleased. "How do you like the taste of raw valkmannon root?"

It actually tasted vaguely of cinnamon and coffee, with perhaps a bit of volcanic loam, not at all unpleasant. But Chance was still not happy with its placement, not only because it prevented him explaining why he was here but also because he could not issue indictments against this unpleasant Harrow-Teaguer.

"Off to find me a Balliope," said the Harrow-Teaguer, standing and donning a greatcoat the size of an infield tarp. "I happen to know Chet Ciric'L'Flon personally."

Why don't you just call him then? thought Chance.

"So no misbehaving while I'm gone. You'll just make things worse for yourself, human."

And with that the Harrow-Teaguer turned out the lights and left, slamming and locking the door behind him.

Chance immediately reached into his pockets with his bound hands, but they had been emptied. He tested the limits of his tether—about a yard. He could stand, but barely. A faint light from a distant room allowed him to see that the tether appeared to be of braided leather, much like his mom's old belts from the 1980s. It was tied in a hard knot to a slender pipe of some kind that ran along a baseboard. Chance leaned, pulled, yanked, to no avail. If his mouth

wasn't full of valkmannon root, he would chew his way through the tether. Though he couldn't see, it felt like whatever was binding his wrists was made of the same braided leather. It was hopelessly secure. Chance began to thrash. He thrashed till he wore himself out. He kicked the throw rug.

It caught on something. He kicked it again. Chance sat on the floor and pushed the throw rug with his feet to investigate the source of the snag.

A nail, sticking out of the floor. Chance spun around on his rear end, tore the throw rug off the nail, and began rasping the bindings on his wrists against the jagged nail. In five minutes he was sweating like crazy, his muscles aching from the exertion and the strange angle. Finally, *snp!* Chance sawed his way through one of the leather plaits, then *twsp!* another, and *rp!* another, and *shlk!* the last one finally gave and Chance was free. He wrenched the valkmannon root from his jaws, then ran to the door, but it was locked. It was large and solid, a Harrow-Teaguer door, the doorknob at eye level and made of solid brass. He could never get through that way. There were no windows.

At least not in this room. Chance ran to what he assumed was the bedroom and turned on the light. The biggest futon Chance had ever seen sat unmade in a corner of the room, old pizza boxes and empty soda bottles surrounding it on the floor. One wall was a mass of dark green blackout curtains. With some difficulty Chance drew them, revealing a

picture window looking out onto Donbaloh and the Yalphala River from perhaps the 400th floor. Chance studied the cityscape, looking for landmarks he recognized, but he saw nothing; he was in a part of town he did not know. Some of the buildings were named: the Fanshaw-Heliopause (a squat, homely structure obviously built on Oppabof brutalist models), Wylp Deb-On-Aire (a cheap-looking motel that resembled a huge Easy-Bake Oven), the Standarde Drop (a solid structure, having much in common with a nineteenth-century bank vault), the Quaring-de-Locq (carved right out of the rock and disappearing thousands of stories into the firmament). Across the river, off in the distance between two dark and forbidding buildings, both unnamed, Chance could see another building and part of its neon sign, which read:—OVER ❦ FED—.

What did Braig say the name of Rougi Fatol's building was? The Undercover Federation Building? Chance thought about it. The more he thought, the more he was sure he was right, that the half-hidden building across the Yalphala River was Rougi's; that was where Chance needed to be.

He looked down. Below him was a balcony with two chairs and a table—occupied by two Vyrndeets playing Scrabble under a floor lantern. As far as he could tell, the Harrow-Teaguer's apartment had no balcony, and the window didn't open. Chance couldn't rightly break the window with the Vyrndeets there; someone could get hurt.

How could he get them off the balcony? Chance turned

on all the lights, roamed the apartment. Everything was so . . . *large*. The chairs, the stereo, the wine cabinet, the sink in the kitchen, the ceilings . . .

Chance looked up. Tacked to the middle of the living room ceiling was a tie-dyed sheet, like one might see in a college dorm. It rippled gently in the frigid air-conditioning. One corner was tied to a familiar object.

A sprinkler. The kind that might be attached to a fire alarm system.

Chance ran to the kitchen, turned a gas burner on high. He opened a slender closet near the refrigerator and found a broom, an antique with an aluminum handle twice as long as Chance was tall with half its bristles missing, the other half clogged with the lint of a messy Harrow-Teaguer's life. Chance stuck the linty bristles in the flame till they kindled, not long at all, then ran into the living room and waved the flambeau under the sprinkler.

Nothing.

Then, the deluge.

The water and the piercing siren seemed to come from everywhere at once, and in an instant Chance was both deaf and soaked. When he recovered, he ran to the bedroom and looked out the window. The Vyrndeets were gone, the Scrabble board overturned on the floor of the balcony, letters scattered everywhere. Clearly, the alarm worked building-wide. Chance had not planned this far ahead and

did not have anything ready with which to break the window. Nothing at hand seemed appropriately sturdy.

Then Chance remembered something. He ran back to the living room, which was now swimming in two inches of water. Chance had to take his fingers out of his ears to grab a bottle—a jeroboam of Domaine de Felice-Yorde 1982, whatever that was—and haul it back to the bedroom, raise it over his head, and charge the window.

Neither broke.

The siren at this point was so dizzyingly loud, Chance thought he might be going crazy. He ran back into the kitchen, found a sponge on the edge of the sink, ripped it in two, and jammed each half in his ears. *Ah.*

Chance then began to rifle through the drawers in the kitchen. Utensils. Receipts. A drawer with nothing but varieties of tape. Aha! Tools. Chance found a chisel and ran back to the bedroom.

He jammed the chisel between the window and its seal and began to pry, working his way around, as though he were lifting the lid off a gallon of paint. He pried and pried, and still the pane of glass remained in place. Chance, against his better judgment, leaned his whole body against it and pushed. Of course, that's when it gave way. Chance, and the massive, Harrow-Teaguer-scale pane of glass, fell out of the building.

Fortunately they landed on the Vyrndeets' balcony. The

glass did not break, but Chance landed on it hard. He stood slowly, rubbing his knee and hip and head. When he was sure he was intact, he opened the sliding glass door to the Vyrndeets' apartment, raced through to the front door and out to the hallway. He turned to look at the number on their door: 432.121. The 432nd floor.

The alarm stopped. Chance ran down the hall looking for an elevator, found the stairs, and took those. He ran down to the 401st floor, then found the elevators to the street and was soon on the banks of the Yalphala River, looking for a way across.

CHAPTER 10

At the demonstration, Pauline had been separated from Braig as she had been separated from her brother, the crowd eventually inexorably squeezing her out a side alley like so much toothpaste. She was utterly lost. She ran until the din was diminished enough that she could at least hear fulgurite communication in her head. She stopped in a dark doorway across from a shuttered noodle shop, closed her eyes, and listened for voices in her head. There was nothing from Chance, but Mersey came in loud and clear.

What's going on down there?

I've got a lead on getting in touch with Tylotch Plariant, the prefect of Donbaloh, who I believe can help us, but I've lost Chance.

What happened?

Pauline detailed the demonstration, the socks, the stampede.

Any developments in Oppabof?

A complication.

Oh no.

I've been reading about Valentine Sleaford. There's more to him than meets the eye.

Oh?

Two Balliopes in uniform, halberds pointing at the sky, came down the alley. They paused in their promenade and eyed Pauline with suspicion.

It turns out Sleaford's something of a philanthropist, something of an economic theorist, something of a visionary. His goals are honorable, his methods Machiavellian.

"Two questions, Ranulphus," said the larger Balliope to the smaller. "One, would you say that the human is loitering, and two, are humans still illegal?"

The smaller, who resembled Winston Churchill crossed with a corduroy sofa bolster, leaned on his halberd and said, "One, I would say the human is the very *definition* of a loiterer, and two, humans are, sadly, now legal."

What do you mean, Mersey? Pauline was having trouble keeping track of two conversations.

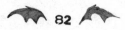

Valentine Sleaford mines to help the poor.

What?

"Humanism may be legal, but loitering is not," said the larger Balliope, taking a step closer to Pauline. She crouched deeper into the doorway.

Most of what he makes he gives away. He believes that gold is evil, responsible for poverty, and mines for it in hopes of finding a vein so large it will devalue the metal worldwide. He's mined all over the Earth, but never in our state, because Texas is not known for gold reserves. Except one county—Presidio. Guess what county Saint Philomene's is under.

Yeah. I get it. Well, he'll get what he's after. They have five thousand cubic meters down here.

Of gold?

"Do we arrest her?"

"No!" said Pauline.

"Why not?"

"According to Donbaloh Civil Practice and Remedies Code Title 5 Section 108.001.(2)(B)," fibbed Pauline, "fines for loitering shall not exceed fifty clahd and are immediately payable to the confronting officer(s), the offense to be commensurately discharged."

Of gold, Mersey. According to the Mifply Currency Exchange.

But they've only ever mined 9261 square meters, total.

How do you know so much?

Oh, facts stick in my head.

Regardless of honorable intentions, we can't let Valentine

Sleaford poke a hole in Donbaloh. According to Braig, the atmospheric differential caused by a breach would kill everything down here.

Maybe somebody could simply tell Valentine that.

That's not a half-bad idea, Mersey.

"How do you know Donbaloh law so well?" said the larger Balliope. "Are you some kind of super attorney?"

"The superest," said Pauline, standing up straight and crossing her arms. "I am a judge in the Fourth Circuit Court of Appeals. Pauline Jeopard presiding! To order, Balliopes!"

The larger Balliope looked impressed, stood at attention, saluted. The smaller one narrowed its eyes and adopted a skeptical countenance. Pauline realized at that moment she was pushing it. The Balliope said:

"There is . . ."

What's happening there, Pauline?

I'm being hassled by the police. I think I'm in trouble.

". . . no appellate court system in Donbaloh."

"Of course there is."

"Our judicial system is based on customary law, and our courts on trial and retrial."

"Heavens, is that the vampire Lestat?"

Pauline pointed beyond the Balliopes. When they turned to look, she took off in the other direction as fast as her legs would take her. She turned a corner, tried the first door she encountered, which opened onto darkness. She ducked

inside, closed the door. She heard the shrieking, cursing Balliopes run past outside, once in one direction, then back the other way. Then they were gone.

A light went on. Pauline turned to behold an elderly creature standing in a doorway on the other side of a small room whose four walls were lined with shelves on which sat dozens of exquisite teapots. Pauline recognized the creature to be a Geckasoft, a delicate E.T.-like being with great healing abilities but itself subject to infirmity.

"My friend, are you lost?" said the Geckasoft, her eyes staring unfocused into the room. Pauline realized she was blind. Pauline thought she'd better be straight up.

"I'm trying to find Tylotch Plariant. Some Balliopes tried to arrest me for loitering, and I hid in here. I'm sorry."

"You sound human."

"I am."

"What is it that you want with Tylotch? I daresay you will not find him here."

The Geckasoft moved slowly to the center of the room and sat at a low table covered with small stones. Pauline realized it was a Go board. How could she play blind?

Pauline found no reason not to tell the Geckasoft about Valentine Sleaford, so she did. She also told her the plan to find Rod Nthn and Rougi Fatol and Darly de Phanxaire.

A thump at the door.

"Just the newspaper," said the Geckasoft. "May I ask you something?"

"Of course."

"Are you the humans that saved Yryssy Ayopy a few months ago?"

"Well . . ."

"She is my cousin. I am Amanda Ayopy. My family is in your debt."

Amanda got up and made her way to the door. She fetched the newspaper, half of which was in a Donbalese version of Braille, the other half in conventional English.

"Won't you stay for tea?"

"I really should go; there's no time to lose."

"Let me at least give you directions to Saint Philomene's."

Pauline left with directions and the newspaper. She caught the Indelarie-Pont Jitney and sat down in the back. She began reading the news of Donbaloh. None of it made any sense whatsoever, except the articles on the riots, which had been going on for several days. She read the sports pages, real estate, comics, classifieds. At the end were the society pages.

TINA KONIUY-POW ENGAGED TO ORNY DEMBANGY'VA'DOSC

JUNOO CRIISPII TO DEBUT AT FLAKKATIO GALA

SALICIA QOPHUT'BHAU ENGAGED TO BARNEY PLUTH

WONYE FREDMAN-MANFRED ENGAGED TO CHURT NEGRUDZE

KRASHI DAUI TO DEBUT AT STANDARDE DROP

DARLY DE PHANXAIRE NOW ELIGIBLE

Pauline sat up. She elbowed the creature sitting next to her, a strange yeti-like beast in a yellow-and-mauve rain slicker.

"Do you know anything about this?" Pauline pointed at the last item.

"Oh yes," said the creature in a voice not unlike Lucille Ball's. "Isn't it exciting? She turned ol' Rougi Fatol loose. Darly's in the market for a husband once again. She told the *Tribune* that Rougi was afraid of commitment."

Mersey, help me.

But Mersey was not there.

CHAPTER 11

Chance wandered up and down the banks of the Yalphala but could find no way across. No bridge, no boat, and swimming was out of the question—the current was too swift, and it was at least four hundred yards from bank to bank. Chance sat on a bench to think.

How did creatures get across? They must need to all the time. They must go under somewhere. Chance looked behind him.

An old, blinking neon sign over an entrance in a building read TREAPHINE TUNNEL.

Chance ran inside, took the spiral staircase two steps

at a time, ran down the tunnel past the trudging populace, up the staircase on the far side of the river, and emerged on the opposite bank. In moments he was standing in the lobby of the Undercover Federation Building, examining the floor directory. The Igneo Lounge where Rougi Fatol worked as a bouncer was on the 854th floor. Chance found an express elevator and was soon at the penthouse. Music thumped down the hall, blue and purple lights pulsed in the dark, and bodies writhed in the misty, humid atmosphere. Chance made his way to a curtained doorway next to which sat a being that looked like a morph of a professional wrestler and an active volcano. He gave Chance a fierce stare. Chance stared fiercely back.

"Rougi Fatol?

The creature's fishy lips moved, obviously saying something, but Chance couldn't hear him.

"What?"

Chance realized at that moment that he still had the sponge wads stuck in his ears. He plucked them out. A great wall of sound assaulted him.

"I said, who wants to know?"

"I'm a friend of Rod Nthn."

"Who?"

"Your friend Rod!"

"Look, I'm not Rougi, pal."

"You're not?" said Chance, crestfallen. "Where is he?"

"Drowning his sorrows."

 89

"What?"

"Didn't you know? His fiancée broke it off. I gave him the night off. He's in the lounge, drinking root beer."

"You're kidding."

"Do I look like a kidder?"

He didn't actually.

"Can I talk to him? It's important. A matter of life and death."

The bouncer stared at Chance for a long time. A line had formed behind him, creatures waiting to get into the Igneo Lounge. Impatient creatures ready to party.

"Hurry it up, human!"

"You're too young for the Igneo," said the bouncer finally. "And you're totally wet."

"Then go in there and send him out to me."

"No. Go away."

Chance started to walk away, then darted under the curtain and into the Igneo Lounge. He lost himself in the pressing throng of contorting bodies. He was immediately reminded of the crowd at the demonstration, the chief differences here being that everyone had a drink in their hand and seemed to be having an awfully good time. Chance spied the bar in the distance. On the way he got stuck between two Vyrndeets in white vinyl minidresses doing the Wave; before he could escape, one of them pinched his cheek.

At the bar were nothing but couples: two massive

Harrow-Teaguers screaming over the music into each other's ears; a pair of Euvyds, their bright blue ears sticking out like fan blades, drinking Shirley Temples and poring over a comic book; a couple of Fauxgres, their arms crossed, backs to each other, obviously in a disagreement of some kind; a brace of Giant Cpulbas, their round, furry bodies radiant in the disco glimmer, drinking something exotic from a bowl the size of an aquarium with glow-in-the-dark silly straws; two creatures of an unknown species that looked like mini-lobsters, apparently claw-wrestling. At the very end of the bar was an unattached patron of the same species as the bouncer.

Chance tapped it on the shoulder. It slowly turned around.

"Rougi Fatol?" Chance screamed.

"Yes?"

"I'd like to buy you a root beer."

Chance had no clahd, but he would worry about that later.

"Oh. Okay. You heard, huh," Rougi screamed over the music.

"I'm sorry."

"Who are you again?"

"Friend of Rod's."

"Oh. Good ol' Rod."

Rougi began to cry. The bartender, a tall, skinny Wreau, put a couple of coasters on the bar.

"Two root beers."

"Start a tab?"

"Huh?"

"You wanna start a tab?"

"Um, okay."

"What's your name?" said Rougi. "And why are you all wet?"

"Name's Chance, sweaty from dancing. Say, Rougi, let's get out of here, go sit down by the river, where we can hear ourselves talk. What do you say?"

"I don't know. I feel safe here."

"C'mon. I bet we could both use a break from the racket in here."

Rougi sighed, a sound like the roar of a furnace.

"Well. Okay."

Chance and Rougi ducked away before the bartender came back with their root beers, squeezed across the dance floor, and left the Igneo Lounge. The bouncer was not in evidence.

Down at street level, Chance's eardrums thrummed. They found a wrought-iron bench along the banks of the Yalphala River and sat.

Chance had absolutely no idea what to say to a heartbroken person. Creature, rather. Chance had no experience with love. All he knew he'd gained secondhand from observing Mersey Marsh. This boy from across town, Cary Bodace, had unceremoniously dumped Mersey after they'd

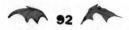

dated for the month of July, and Mersey had gone on a lot of crying jags in Pauline's room, real sinus-reamers. Then one day she was fine, and before long she met Killiam Ng.

"It'll be okay, you know," said Chance, patting Rougi on his massive shoulder.

"No, no, it won't."

Chance was mindful of his prime directive, which was not consoling Rougi Fatol, but finding Darly de Phanxaire and Tylotch Plariant.

"You might have a rough month, but then it'll be all over, and you'll meet someone new."

"But I don't *want* someone new, I want *Darly!*"

Chance held his breath.

"You can tell me what happened if you want."

Rougi was quiet for a long time. The Yalphala sped along in a low hush, creatures now and then leaping out of the water, twisting and shining in the city glare, and splashing back into the racing current.

"There's not much to tell. I blame it all on *Pie Taster, Pie Master*, a self-help book by this Vyrndeet named Binsome Jukkop. It's all about not letting people drag you down on your journey to wealth and self-actualization. Darly took a seminar with Binsome and evidently got it into her head that I was dragging her down. Rougi Fatol, lowly, uneducated bouncer, going nowhere. I don't think Binsome convinced her to dump me, but he didn't discourage her. And here we are."

"Let's go win her back."

"What?"

"Let's make a list of your good points and bowl her over."

"I don't know."

Chance went for it.

"Where is she now?"

"With Tylotch somewhere, probably."

"Can you call her?"

"I guess."

"What's your greatest attribute, Rougi? And remember, now is no time to be modest. We are fighting for your life, here."

Chance made a list of Rougi's greatest strengths. They crafted language to convince Darly of Rougi's worthiness as a boyfriend. Chance coached Rougi in the subtleties of body language and how to communicate humility, respect, and patience. In an hour, they were ready. Rougi made the call.

"Darly, it's me, Rougi."

"—"

"Yes."

"—"

"I'd like to see you one last time."

"—"

"I'll be brief."

"—"

"No, no. I won't make trouble. I'll come to you. Where are you?"

 94

"—"

"All right. See you soon."

Chance couldn't believe his luck. He was going to get to meet Tylotch Plariant!

"What'd she say?"

"She'll meet me. Thanks for all your help, Chance. I'll let you know how it goes."

"Wait—can't I go with you? You might need me."

"I can't let you come along because she's with Tylotch. Matter of realm security, et cetera."

"Oh. I see. Well, good luck, Rougi. I'll leave you to it."

Chance turned to go. He walked along the Yalphala a ways, watching Rougi in the reflection of the glass of his watch. Rougi ducked into the Treaphine Tunnel going under the river. Chance turned and ran after him. Careful not to get too close, Chance followed Rougi as he resurfaced on the other side and walked down a street between two towering stone buildings. He came to an intersection and stopped, Chance a few dozen yards behind him in the shadows. Presently, a streetcar approached and slowed. Rougi climbed on, and the streetcar began to accelerate. Chance ran after it, caught a rung, and climbed on the back. Mercifully no ticket collector came along. Keeping his head down low, Chance kept an eye on Rougi near the front of the car.

They made numerous stops before Rougi finally jumped off and began walking briskly into a dark part of the realm

populated with scary-looking creatures and obscure businesses. He stopped at a very slender building of pink granite guarded by Harrow-Teaguers in black suits. It was the sort of modern structure that had the elevators on the outside of the building. Rougi conferred with the Harrow-Teaguers for a moment before they allowed him inside. Soon Rougi appeared in an elevator. Chance concentrated on counting the floor it stopped on . . . 1, 2, 3, 4, 5, 6, 7, 8, 9, 10, 11, 12, 13, 14, 15, 16 . . . 16.

Tylotch Plariant was on the sixteenth floor!

But which room?

And how would he get past those Harrow-Teaguers?

CHAPTER 12

Mersey Marsh had been working as a cat sitter that summer and had accumulated more than a thousand bucks scooping litter boxes and scraping cat barf off linoleum floors. She had also gotten her driver's license, admittedly after a couple of tries, that pesky hedge foiling her parallel-parking attempt the first time, and the second time the driving test judge not giving her a break on the five-point turn. But no matter, she was a licensed driver now, and since Killiam had a diving meet in Starling and couldn't go anywhere, she would be traveling out to Presidio County in his truck to find Valentine Sleaford on her own.

Killiam's old Ford had no air-conditioning, so Mersey dressed in her most lightweight black outfit and abandoned makeup altogether. She assembled a cooler of sandwiches and bottles of ice tea and water and seedless grapes and plenty of ice. She bought a phone charger that stuck in the car lighter and a folding map in case she lost the GPS signal. She had three hundred in cash, a debit card, Venmo and PayPal accounts on her phone, and another debit card hidden under the seat of the truck. Driving time to Rincón Oscuro was about four and a half hours. She told her parents she was going to protest a fracking site in West Texas, so there was at least a grain of truth to her story. Her parents, Francine and Hix Marsh, had not known their daughter to have a political streak, but any variation on the black arts was okay with them, so they consented, as long as Killiam shared the driving. Mersey assured them he would. She set out, alone, at four fifteen in the morning, before the sun rose and began to boil the dew off the land.

Sometime before nine a.m. Mersey found herself on Orange Street, the main thoroughfare of Rincón Oscuro. She pulled into a parking space in front of the Mercury Café, the only place that seemed to be open for business. Inside she sat at a booth looking out over Orange Street and waited for someone to notice her. The café was utterly empty, but two brimming globes of coffee sat steaming on a Bunn coffeemaker behind the counter: Someone was here.

Mersey wasn't really all that hungry, but she could use some coffee. She liked it black, of course.

She stood up, walked behind the counter, found a mug on the drainboard, filled it to the top, and went back to her booth. She took a sip. It was darn good.

A waitress emerged from somewhere. Her hair was parted on the side and fell over one eye. She looked up, did a double take when she saw Mersey, then composed herself, produced a pencil from a pouch at her waist, and used it to push her hair out her eye. She smiled and marched over to Mersey's booth, two menus in hand—lunch and dessert.

"Hi and welcome to the Mercury, I see you have your coffee already, can I bring you a Coke or a Dr Pepper while you're looking over the menus?"

"I think I know what I want," said Mersey, without even touching the menus. Mersey had spent a fair part of her life in Dairy Queens and cognate establishments, and was familiar with their fare. "Biscuits, side of bacon—crispy, please—and a banana split, no nuts."

"Fudge?"

"Yes, please."

"You got it."

Mersey watched the sparse traffic on Orange Street: a crimson El Camino with tinted windows and two enormous hogs in the bed, obviously in no particular hurry; a slate-blue Volvo drawing a shiny Airstream trailer; a yellow-and-black

Corvette that made Mersey think of wasps; an old diesel Mercedes the color of green dish soap.

The waitress brought Mersey's order.

"Can you tell me how to find Miss Frieda Bull Radegast? The Lazy Yucca Ranch?"

The waitress, who up till this point had been affable and laid-back, froze up.

"Oh, um. Well. I'm not . . . I can't—"

"No," said a voice.

Mersey looked up. A tall man with skin the warm hue of medium-roast coffee beans was walking toward her booth. He looked like a Texas Ranger—big balsa-wood-colored felt Stetson, dusty Nocona boots, pressed Dickies. Shaved so close he must've used a samurai sword. Thumbs hitched in his belt loops. Buckle like a turkey platter. Mersey stared.

"No what?" she said after a moment.

"The Lazy Yucca Ranch," he said, shifting a toothpick from one side of his mouth to the other, "is not open to visitors."

Mersey Marsh chose to ignore him. Mersey Marsh was an excellent ignorer. It felt bad to be ignored by Mersey, no matter who you were, even if you were a larger-than-life Texan with dusty boots and an attitude to match.

"Who are you?" he said.

Mersey ignored him.

"I'm Carver Hebert."

Nobody moved, except Mersey, who dug into her weird breakfast.

"You might as well go on back where you came from, now."

Mersey thought this was some of the best bacon she'd ever had.

"You heard me?" said Carver Hebert.

Out the window Mersey saw a Cadillac Escalade pickup stop at the intersection of Orange and Escondido. The angle of the morning sun prevented her from seeing the driver. The vehicle idled for a moment, then turned right. Mersey could just make out its Texas vanity plate:

ALL MINE

She thought about this for half a second, then reached into her purse for her billfold, found a twenty, left it on the table, slid out of the booth, sidled past Carver Hebert with his hands on his hips, and sauntered coolly out of the Mercury Café, her cheeks still full of biscuit.

At first, Killiam's old Ford threatened not to start, but it gave in and turned over at last, and Mersey was soon on Escondido, heading north. Before long, the Escalade appeared on the horizon, and she followed at a safe distance. After a few miles the Escalade turned off onto a dirt road guarded with NO TRESPASSING and PRIVATE PROPERTY signs, rumbled over a cattle guard, and disappeared behind

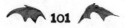

a low hill. Mersey paused at the turnoff for a moment, then followed. At the top of the hill she stopped.

Below her, in a shallow valley, a small mining operation was in full force. Four huge Bucyrus RH400 excavators were at work—Sleaford meant business. The Escalade was parked next to a single-wide trailer.

Mersey left her truck where it was and walked down to the trailer. She knocked on the door. Valentine Sleaford aka Neville Fred Antaso answered the door. His lower jaw fell like a cannonball dropped from the Leaning Tower of Pisa.

"Mersey!"

"Yes, Valentine. We need to talk. Do you have air-conditioning in there?"

"Er, yes. Come in."

There was a golf tournament on TV.

"So that wasn't an act. You really like golf."

"Look, my deception was all for a greater good."

Valentine briefly explained his theory of poverty and how he could defeat it by compromising gold values.

"I respect that," said Mersey. "But I'm here to educate you about the destruction you are about to wreak by the actual mining. Do you realize there are eleven *million* creatures, sentient beings, down there that will perish if you breach the surface, if their atmosphere and our atmosphere mix? Chance and Pauline are down there now, and they have been unable to contact the leader, who is a bit of

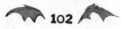

a paranoid nut. So, if you break through, all those creatures will die. Is that worth it?"

Valentine sat down. He picked up the remote control and flipped idly through the channels on TV. Then he turned it off. Nothing but the sound of the window unit broke the silence, and the distant roar of the excavators.

Valentine said, "I can do nothing but play the numbers here, Mersey. Eleven million is a great many, um, creatures, but I stand to save so many more by reducing poverty worldwide."

"You don't know that your gold theory will reduce poverty. You don't even know if there's gold down there. What we do know is that breaking through the stone sky of Donbaloh will kill the subterranean populace."

"I am confident in my theory, my calculations, my computer modeling, Mersey. I am confident there is gold down there; there has always been gold in Presidio County."

"So how can I convince you to abandon your mining project?"

"I'm doing the right thing."

"What did you think of Chance? Of Pauline? Did you care for them? Or was that an act, too?"

"No, no, I love them, and it devastated me to leave them, but you have to understand what we are up against, and that this is the great scourge of the world. Poverty, Mersey."

"Well, Chance and Pauline cannot get out of Donbaloh without the help of the locals. And if the locals are dead,

then my friends will eventually perish, too. And it will be your fault."

Valentine Sleaford, who had been standing in a stream of air-conditioning at one end of the trailer, suddenly sat down on a greenish-brown La-Z-Boy recliner and put his head in his hands.

"Sleaford, the United States and most of the rest of the world has been off the gold standard for a long time. Gold doesn't matter that much. I think your theory is misguided."

"You're wrong, Mersey," said Valentine, jumping up, suddenly animated. "Gold is a *psychological* matter. It is the cardinal motivating substance of the world, and has been for millennia. Nothing else even comes close. But gold devastates at one hundred times the rate at which it enriches. The only solution to this is to flood the market with so much of it that no one wants it anymore. Donbaloh offers this possibility. It is my duty to investigate."

"And if you're wrong?" said Mersey, pointing at Valentine's nose, her green eyes blazing. "Eleven million and two, dead?"

Valentine looked defiant.

"The odds are in my favor, and I'm taking the bet."

"Sleaford, I have an idea. Why don't you put the big machines in park, pay a visit to Donbaloh, and just see how much gold there actually is, if any. I know how to get in."

Valentine looked thoughtful and suspicious at the same time.

"How?"

"Well, admittedly it's not easy. You have to swim more than one hundred feet in an underwater tunnel, then paddle down a rapid-y river. Once you arrive, you have to find someone to show you around, which might be tricky."

"Can't swim, hate boats, loathe tourism. Won't work, Mersey."

"Then send a minion! You must have a gajillion employees."

"Don't trust them not to just grab a few bars of gold and disappear."

"So you are refusing?"

"Yes."

Mersey stared. She decided to say something she had absolutely no way of backing up, something for which she had no plan formulated.

"You are forcing me to resort to extreme measures."

"Really, Mersey? Are you a friend to poverty?"

"Oh, so it's like that."

A knock came at the door. Three sharp raps, perhaps accomplished with a knuckle, followed by two softer, slower thumps, likely performed with the flat of a fist. Obviously an identifying knock.

"That would be my right-hand man, Mr.—"

"Let me guess. Carver Hebert."

"You must've stopped at the Mercury. That's his hangout."

"Are you going to invite him in?"

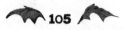

Valentine opened the door for Carver, who was so tall he had to duck to enter. He took off his beige hat and held it to his chest. The sun was so blinding outside it clearly was taking his eyes a moment to adjust to the darkness in the room, and he didn't immediately notice Mersey. When he did, he performed a slight bow.

"Good morning, ma'am. I tried to follow you, but my old Pontiac doesn't do so well in this heat. Otherwise you wouldn't have made it out to your rendezvous with Mr. Sleaford here."

Carver Hebert sounded genuinely contrite, as though his job had been to protect her from Valentine, not the other way around. In any case it was time for Mersey to take her leave.

Then she had an idea.

"Carver, would you exterminate eleven million people if it meant you could have a chance, say a one-in-ten chance, of eradicating poverty? No guarantees—a gamble."

Carver seemed to think about this.

"Why, no, I would not."

"Why?"

"Once you are dead, you are dead. Even if you are living in poverty, you are still alive. Life is precious."

"Just so you know, your boss over there is taking that gamble. Maybe you can talk some sense into him."

The two men looked at each other, then down at the threadbare carpet.

Mersey strode over and shook Carver's hand; it felt like squeezing a catcher's mitt. Then she stepped back and walked over to Valentine Sleaford. She gave him a sly smile, then a quick hug, clearly surprising him.

"Good luck, Sleaford," she said. "You're going to need it."

Then Mersey Marsh turned on her heel, left the trailer, and walked back to Killiam Ng's truck.

CHAPTER 13

As the Indelarie-Pont Jitney rumbled through Donbaloh on its way to Saint Philomene's Infirmary, Pauline reassessed her position:

1. Rougi Fatol might no longer have any value if Darly de Phanxaire had broken up with him. And so finding Rod Nthn might not be the best course of action.
2. She had misplaced her brother.
3. Balliopes still seemed to be a threat.
4. Time was running out.

What to do?

Pauline looked around at all the creatures on the jitney and suddenly felt very lonesome. She had brought her little brother along on a fool's errand, and now she had gone and lost him. Moreover, she had deceived her mother in the process. What could Daisy be thinking right now? Had she missed them? Or was she oblivious, thinking Pauline and Chance were at their Uncle Jones's, petting baby goats and eating pimento cheese sandwiches and watching old VHS cassette recordings of *Space: 1999* with Barbara Bain and Martin Landau?

Across from Pauline sat an elderly Euvyd, a quite human-looking species with bright blue ears and transparent hair. It gave Pauline a kind smile and a nod. Pauline wondered briefly about *its* mother; then she quietly began to cry. Pauline hid her face in the newspaper as tears ran down her cheeks. When she could no longer stand the tickle of tears on her skin, she wiped them away with the newspaper. She wondered if she had left smears of newsprint on her face. She decided she didn't care. When she looked up, the Euvyd was gone; in fact the entire car was vacant. She imagined all the creatures wandering home to their mothers.

Pauline had a thought.

The jitney entered a tunnel and fifteen minutes later came to a stop in a large roundabout lined on one side with a bank of elevators.

"End of the line!" some creature shouted. "Sa-a-a-a-aint Philomene's In-n-n-n-nfirmare-e-e-e-e!"

Two elevator rides later and Pauline was at Rod Nthn's door. She knocked.

No answer.

She knocked again, waited. She tried the door, and it opened. Pauline went in.

"Rod? It's me, Pauline."

No response.

Pauline looked around for Rod's computer, which was what she had come for. *Ah, that must be it,* a primitive-looking desktop in the corner on a table made of solid gold. It took her a moment to power it up, but eventually the screen came to life. His screen saver was of the Esteemed Librarian in front of a wall of books. The keyboard was entirely unfamiliar, but in time Pauline found the Donbaloh internet version of Google and searched for Tylotch Plariant's mother.

Come to find out her name was Fiolepta Plariant, and she lived at 568.145 Jaulareo Bulster, a towering building in the west end of Donbaloh. From what Pauline could gather, Fiolepta lived alone with her four charls, furry, cat-like pets with three legs that have the ability to hum beautiful melodies of their own devising. Pauline then pulled up the jitney map and found the best route to Jaulareo Bulster.

Before she left, she found Rod's phone.

"Directory assistance, how may I direct your call?"

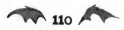

"Braig Toop."

"You've gotta be kidding me."

"C'mon, just put the call through."

Pauline was in no mood for attitude.

"Hello?"

"Braig."

"Pauline, are you all right?"

"Fine, is Chance with you?"

"No, I was hoping he was with you."

"We got separated at the protest."

"Any fulgurite transmissions?"

"Not a thing. I'm worried."

"Did you read about Darly?"

"Yeah." For reasons that were unclear even to her, Pauline didn't want to tell Braig about Fiolepta. Maybe she was afraid he would tell her the idea was foolish, and she would be left with no plan of action.

"Do you want to come by and regroup?" said Braig.

"I think time is running out; I'm going to think on the run."

"Let me know if I can help. And check in with me periodically in case I hear from your brother."

"Will do. Bye for now, Braig. Perhaps you and your family and friends should evacuate."

"Pauli—"

But she was already out the door.

Back on the jitney Pauline tried to contact Mersey and Chance, without success. She changed for the Cange-Nalcocatches Line and promptly fell asleep, until a terrible bang awakened her. The jitney came to a stop. Presently a conductor, a short Vyrndeet in a red velvet uniform, came down the aisle and announced that the jitney was out of order, that everyone was to disembark.

"You can either wait here, and a replacement will be along in an hour or so, or you can hazard Serialto Park yonder, through which one can meet with a jitney on the Dinff-Ilcx Line after a mere fifteen-minute walk."

A narrow path led into Serialto Park, a dark, forbidding tangle of vast, root-like, leafless trees, thick beds of ivy with strange black flowers, and odd cattails that oscillated like metronomes, not to mention dozens of other weird flora, all of which seemed quite sentient, aware of what came and went in the park they all called home.

Not a single traveler from the jitney made a move toward the park. Pauline found there was no time to lose and headed straight for the entrance.

Something about Serialto Park made her feel unwelcome. But she entered anyway. The cattails accelerated in their metronomic back-and-forthing; a faint clicking could be heard. The deeper she penetrated the park, the darker it got, the cooler the air became, the narrower the path grew. Pauline sensed intelligent malevolence all around her. She looked up.

A huge, thick tree covered in scaly red bark and hung with odd, perfectly spherical cannonball-black fruit spread over Pauline. Up in the branches small creatures like metallic ferrets chased one another about. One creature leaped onto a piece of fruit, and, in jumping off, dislodged it, and it fell to the ground, broke open on contact, and released, along with an odor related to but far worse than sulfur dioxide, a flurry of small, wriggling, yellow-and-pink-striped, worm-like creatures, some of which hit Pauline in the face and landed in her hair. She shrieked and ran into the botanical Hades, whipping her red curls about and raking her fingers through her hair, until she came to a stop in a small clearing. She carefully checked herself for those monstrous worm-seeds, and, finding no more, sat down to catch her breath. She began to question her decision to come through Serialto Park.

Above Pauline the strange metallic ferrets jumped and flew and flicked their tails; below her the ground was alive with four-legged insects and twisting, fawn-colored worms the size of crayons; and all around her grew exquisitely monstrous plants, some of which would occasionally uncoil a frond and reach out for her.

Pauline stepped on something that did not feel like soil. It felt rather like a welcome mat. She looked down just as what appeared to be a dirt-brown elastic curtain began to rise all around her, its edges lifting as though by invisible strings, until she was entirely enclosed, sealed off as if she

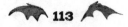

113

were in a huge, rubber drawstring pouch. The plant began to lift her off the ground, causing the walls to draw more tightly around her, until only a single point of light directly above her shone faintly in her eyes. She had walked into a kind of colossal Venus flytrap, a tarp-sized leaf hidden in the dirt that had snared her like a lion as she walked across it. She scratched viciously at the leaf, but the strong, elastic walls resisted all assault.

All at once Pauline noticed the odor of burning rubber. She stood perfectly still.

The sound of running liquid. At her feet. Beginning to slowly fill the pouch. It was somehow melting the rubber soles of her shoes.

Pauline was being digested.

She screamed, but from the muffled resound she could tell that very little noise could escape this horrible pouch, especially the terrified cries of a human. Soon the liquid would eat through the rubber and leather of her shoes and begin to dissolve her feet. She reached as high as she could, but the circle of light was at least two feet above her. There was nothing for her to get a grip on to begin climbing. She went through her pockets. Ah, her pocketknife! But just as she got it open, she dropped it, and it splashed in the caustic, gathering liquid. Her mini flashlight was of no use except to illuminate the deteriorating shape of her shoes and the choking smoke or steam or whatever it was that was rising from them.

Pauline began to panic. She did not like enclosed spaces at all. At least she wasn't upside down, her head being eaten away by floral acids.

"Mersey!"

But Mersey didn't answer. The unpredictability of the fulgurite walkie-talkies was beginning to outstrip their usefulness. Mersey, in fact—

Pauline thought of something. She gathered up some of the pouch like the scruff of a dog's neck, prepared herself for what would surely be the worst taste experience of her life, opened her jaws wide, and bit the plant.

From somewhere came an excruciated *eeee*, and the walls of the plant began to ripple. Then the pouch started to constrict. Pauline bit it again. It tasted a bit like mandarin oranges and old pretzels. She tore at it with all her might, and the plant screamed and rippled, tightening even more. Pauline took one more bite, chomping down as hard as she could, growling like a dog straining on a leash. Then she lifted up her feet, her full weight now borne by just the strength of her jaws clamped around a scruff of the plant's surface.

It tore. The wall of the plant ripped open as though it had been unzipped. The plant's *eeee*-ing doubled in magnitude. The hole she'd made was too small for her to crawl through, so she ripped again, this time accidentally splashing the digestive juices on her bare ankle.

"Aah!" she yelled. It was as if her skin were being peeled

off like a sticker. Trying to ignore the pain, she began to climb out of the hole she'd created. Once she got her head and shoulders through, she looked down—the pouch hung nearly thirty feet above the ground from a long vine attached to a tree branch. She'd break her legs, or worse, if she fell that far.

Suddenly there was a searing pain in her big toe. The acid had eaten through her shoes. She struggled to work the rest of her body past the tear, at the same time kicking her shoes and socks off and allowing them to fall back into the acrid digestive soup. Finally she wriggled her way all the way out and found herself holding on to the vine for dear life. She couldn't let go. But she couldn't hold on forever, either.

Pauline started to sway back and forth, back and forth, and finally the pouch hanging from its vine began to swing, short arcs, becoming longer and longer, until she was swinging as high as the branch that held the vine, one more swing and she let go and allowed her momentum to carry her into the thick, bushy tufts of leaves of a neighboring tree, through which she gently fell, bouncing from branch to branch, until she was only ten feet from the ground. She hung from the lowest branch, then let go, falling into the soft dirt, barefoot. Above her the horrible, torn plant pouch swinging on its vine began to twist and crumple, shrinking to a tenth of its former size and turning a shade of red-black that Pauline associated with rot and death, until it detached

itself from the vine and fell to the ground, splitting and splattering like an overripe melon.

Pauline ran down the winding path, as fast as she could go without shoes, until at last she emerged onto a normal city sidewalk (such as they were in Donbaloh) with pedestrians, garbage cans, mailboxes, telephone booths—sweet sights for sore eyes. And there, before her, the Dinff-Ilcx Jitney just taking off down the street. She ran, leaped on, found a seat between twin Ult Thivish girls in baby-blue pinafores, crossed her arms, and tried not to think about how much her feet hurt.

CHAPTER 14

The pink granite building was built right into the stone of the Earth, so there was no back entrance—the only way in was past the Harrow-Teaguers guarding the door. Chance would have to play poker. He practiced his most determined and imperious look, and just as he was about to emerge from the shadows, an elevator rose to the sixteenth floor, collected a passenger, and delivered him to the lobby. He emerged onto the street. It was Rougi, looking peaceful and relaxed. He was holding a yellow book.

Chance waited till Rougi disappeared, then strode

purposefully across the street to the entrance of the building, which Chance noticed was called the Mingledari Skybond.

"Out of my way, Harrow-Teaguers!" shouted Chance. "I have an appointment with Tylotch Plariant."

"Whoa, human boy, not so fa-a-a-st," said the larger Harrow-Teaguer, reaching out and grabbing Chance by the shoulder.

"Ow!"

"What makes you think Tylotch Plariant is here?"

"He *told* me he was here. Besides, how many buildings in Donbaloh need guarding by outsize Harrow-Teaguers in penguin suits?"

"Kid has a point, Arnolph."

"When's your appointment?"

"Now."

"What room is he in?"

"Are you kidding?" said Chance. "I'm not telling you that. What if you don't know and you're trying to steal that information from me so you can assassinate him?"

"Kid has another point, Arnolph."

"Shut up, Issydrah."

"If I'm late to my appointment," said Chance, feeling optimistic, "I will make sure to let Tylotch know it was Arnolph and Issydrah who were at fault."

"Look, we can't just let you in."

"I have an idea. What if I identify the floor he's on. That should be enough to prove my business here today."

Arnolph and Issydrah looked at each other.

"Go for it, kid. The Mingledari Skybond has seven hundred thirty floors. Guess which one he's on and we'll let you in."

"The sixteenth."

"Ooh, close, but no dice. Actually the seventeenth. So why don't you run along now, little human, before we eat you."

Arnolph and Issydrah began to laugh, deep, plangent, frightening rumbles.

Chance was dumbfounded. How in the world could he have miscounted?

Next door to the Mingledari Skybond was the Ivrardus Lodge, a motel. Chance made his way into the lobby, which was appointed in greens and golds, with strange potted plants in every corner. There was no one at the desk. A bank of elevators dominated one wall. He pressed DOWN. The doors to a car immediately slid open.

Chance was reminded of the elevators at Saint Philomene's, with their hundreds and hundreds of buttons. This car had 626.

He noticed that it skipped the number 11.

Clearly some unlucky Donbaloh number, like how some Oppaboffian buildings omitted the thirteenth floor. Obviously the source of his floor-counting error.

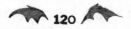

Chance pressed SB, presumably for subbasement. The doors opened onto a dank floor with a low, rough-hewn rock ceiling lined with clanking, dripping pipes shedding their insulation. Along one wall was a small-gauge rail on which were several wheeled hampers. Chance heard a sudden *floonth*, and a big wad of laundry fell from a chute into a hamper. On each of the hampers was stenciled:

hy-gotch mangle and launder

Chance got closer, peered down the length of the rail. There were dozens of laundry hampers, and the rail seemed to extend for hundreds of yards in both directions—it must service every building on the street.

Including the Mingledari Skybond. Chance followed the rail along the wall until he was under the neighboring building. He peeked around the corner. Sure enough, there was a Harrow-Teaguer guarding the elevator. They weren't messing around with security. Of course, this one appeared to be asleep. Chance tiptoed over to a laundry hamper and climbed in. He peered up into the chute above him, listened: nothing. He carefully hoisted himself up and into the chute and began to climb, using tiny fingerholds in the smooth metal siding and the rubber soles of his sneakers for traction. Slowly Chance made his way skyward. His own body blocked the meager light coming from the opening, and it got darker and darker as he climbed, inch by inch. Soon he

was in total blackness. It was silent as a tomb. He paused to rest.

He sensed all at once a . . . *change* in his immediate environment. He could describe it no more accurately to himself than as a shift in the air pressure. Chance noticed a breeze coming from above. A warm, gentle push of atmosphere, a god breathing down his neck. Then Chance realized what it was, and he realized it too late.

Laundry.

A huge wad of dirty laundry traveling forty-five miles per hour down the chute struck Chance and washed him out of the opening like a spider in a drain-spout, landing him in a hamper.

He was not certain if he was more furious or grossed out. Chance was pretty much both. The laundry seemed to comprise dozens of dirty tablecloths, old Donbalese food stains everywhere, and smelled like the inside of an empty soup can. Chance unburied himself and looked up into the chute, as though waiting for another round of laundry from the chute-cannon. Nothing came.

With a combination of alacrity and caution, Chance climbed back up in the chute, scaling as fast as he could, praying that no more laundry comets would punch him in the head.

After what felt like about three stories, a thin line of bright light appeared in the wall of the chute. Chance braced himself against the wall and investigated with his fingertips.

He got purchase on a lip of metal just above the light and lifted. A panel slid upward, revealing the red, green, and brown color scheme of a floor of the Mingledari Skybond. Chance squeezed through, falling onto the floor. He looked around; no creatures were in evidence. As he ran down the hall, heading for the glass elevators at the end of the building, he passed a tray on the floor with the remains of someone's room service: a huge triangle of toast with a fanged bite taken out of the center, a carafe of coffee or whatever, two upturned, unused water glasses. Chance grabbed a water glass.

The elevators. He was evidently on the third floor. He pressed UP. The elevator arrived, and he pressed 17. Sure enough, there was no eleventh floor. Curses! All that laundry nonsense, simply because he hadn't known a Donbaloh superstition.

Chance looked down at the two Harrow-Teaguers guarding the building. He hugged the inside of the elevator in case they chose that moment to look up and foil all his plans.

On the seventeenth floor, Chance got to work immediately. He placed the water glass against the first door he came to, pressed his ear to the bottom, and listened.

". . . circular storms predicted in the Northwest Corridor of Donbaloh through the weekend, small craft advisory in effect for that per . . ."

A television, tuned to a weather channel. Chance moved to the next door and listened with his glass.

"... *Zxxxxsnrrkkllllblpblpblpblpprrrrr* ..."

Some creature with terrible sleep apnea, snoring. Chance moved to the next door.

"*My* lotion!"

"*Mine*, you stole it!"

"Mom gave it to me; I'm the favorite!"

"I'll put your pet quilpheke in the smasher!"

Children. Chance wondered what *kind* of children, what a quilpheke was, what a smasher was *supposed* to smash. On to the next door.

"'Whether 'tis nobler in the mind to suffer / The slings and arrows of fortune'—No, '*outrageous* fortune'—why can't I remember that? Try again ... 'Whether 'tis nobler in the mind to suffer / The slings and arrows of outrageous fortune, / Or to take sea against arms of—' No, no, no, no, *no!*"

Chance couldn't believe it—the only lines of Shakespeare he recognized, and here they were being rehearsed by an actor in Donbaloh, whom he could picture tearing his hair out.

Chance moved to the next door, placed the lip of the water glass against the smooth surface and his ear to the bottom. He listened.

Silence at first. Then faint music, as if from a station on the low end of the AM dial of a portable radio. Then a deep, gravelly voice, male:

"Pack."

"We just got here." Also gravelly, but finer gravel, decidedly feminine.

"We're going to Safe House 8051680-456, in the Bolinjie'Yound District. Haven't spent time there in a while."

"Maybe it's been exposed. You know there's a website of known safe houses."

"So check it."

A moment passed, and only the faint music could be heard.

"Apparently okay. A safe safe house."

"Good."

"I need a shower."

"What's stopping you?"

"I don't know why I work for you."

Chance was still not 100 percent sure this was who he thought it was. He needed more.

"I would make certain you never worked again if you left me."

"Always the charmer, Tylotch."

Bingo.

Chance had already rehearsed what he was going to say.

He knocked on the door.

CHAPTER 15

Back at the Mercury Café, Mersey Marsh sat in what was now her regular booth, and while she waited for the waitress to bring her a Dr Pepper and an order of fries, Mersey watched the front door for Carver Hebert.

He entered at precisely high noon.

"Why don't you have a seat, Mr. Hebert, and choose something off the menu at my expense. I'd like to speak with you for a moment."

Carver Hebert stood in the middle of the restaurant, looking highly amused at the gumption of this sixteen-year-old high school girl. But he slid into the booth and picked up a menu.

"Triple MercBurger, extra avocado, jack cheese, and grilled onion, hold the sissy sauce, double side of fries, large strawberry malted, RC Cola, no ice. Please."

"What I said to Valentine was not hypothetical, Mr. Hebert. If he breaks through, he will kill eleven million intelligent creatures, plus my two friends. That can't happen. Do you understand that?"

Carver Hebert remained mute. He seemed to be balancing loyalty with ethics.

"And if you're a human being," she added, "if you have any kind of compassion, you're going to help me stop him."

"But how, Miss Marsh? I can't rightly tell Mr. Sleaford what to do. He'd just send me packing."

"Does he take any medication?"

"Why, just some vitamins."

"Any capsules?"

Carver put his big head in one hand, looked up at the brim of his hat, and began drumming his fingertips on the table.

"Well, yes, the vitamin B6 he takes is a big ol' maize-and-blue capsule. Go Blue!"

"When does he take it?"

"Morning. Big handful of 'em."

Mersey removed her fulgurite necklace. Using the

Tabasco bottle on the table, she snapped off a piece of fulgurite. She broke it into five or six small pieces and scooped the fragments into a napkin.

"Replace the contents of a B6 capsule with these little mineral chips. Squeeze a little superglue into the capsule to consolidate, reassemble. Arrange it so he swallows the capsule. When he does, let me know."

Mersey wrote her number on the napkin.

"I'm sorry, but I won't let you poison him; that's against the rules."

"I'm not poisoning him."

"Prove it."

Mersey chipped off another fragment of fulgurite and swallowed it with a swig of Dr Pepper.

"Okay?"

"What's gonna happen if he eats superglue?" said Carver.

"As long as it's dried, cyanoacrylate is totally harmless. You can google it if you want."

"What does all this do?"

"I'll be able to reach him telepathically for a short period. Here, wear my necklace for a minute."

See?

Oh dear.

A little unsettling, isn't it?

I'm going to hand this back to you now.

"My two friends and I all have these minerals, called

 128

fulgurites. We'll be able to communicate with Sleaford, and hopefully convince him to stop his mining campaign. If a voice is urging you, directly, in your head, it is harder to resist."

"Miss Marsh, given the nature of the human gastrointestinal tract, you would have twelve hours or so to communicate with him, no more—"

"Yes."

"You think you can convince him?"

"I don't know. Meanwhile, I want you to try to persuade him on your own that what he's doing is wrong."

The waitress brought Carver's Triple MercBurger, fries, and beverages.

"Are you two planning a heist?" she said, a gleam in her eye. She might have been in Rincón Oscuro a little too long, waitressing in a diner a day too many.

"No, dear," said Carver. "We're planning to save a world."

CHAPTER 16

Y ou're ble-e-e-e-eding!" shouted the twin Ult Thivish girls, pointing at Pauline's feet. Where was their mother? Where was the discipline? How long till the Ohf-dey-Lootn stop, where she was due to change jitneys?

"Yes, I know. I was nearly eaten by a carnivorous tree in Serialto Park."

"Ooh, the Intermediate Zampoglio Weed!" said one of the twins. "How did you get caught? They're so easy to avoid."

"I was . . . distracted, let's say," said Pauline, nonplussed. "Intermediate?"

"There are Diminutive and Outsize Zampoglio Weeds," said the other twin. "Outsize can catch and eat a Kenicki-Quither. That, if you don't know, is a creature three times the size of an Oppaboffian African elephant. Kenicki-Quithers are very pleasant and harmless."

"I see."

"You know you're risking a serious fine going barefoot like that," said the twins together.

"Really? Why?"

"Technically, it's because you're not wearing a left sock. It's a new tax handed down by our prefect. Do you have any money? There's a shoe store at Ohf-dey-Lootn."

"I have one hundred sixteen clahd."

"That'll get you socks and some of those sandals Euvyds wear."

Both Ult Thivish girls screwed up their faces and began giggling. The jitney came to a shuddering stop.

"This is us! Good luck, human!"

Pauline jumped off the jitney at Ohf-dey-Lootn and began looking around. Hundreds of little shops lined the streets: butcher shops, stores that sold nothing but strange games, carpet purveyors, junk shops, antiquarian bookstores, soup vendors, places that sold things that Pauline simply could not identify . . . but no shoe stores.

She spied two Balliopes coming toward her, so she ducked into a pet shop. She wandered around, looking at the strange creatures—charls, dewpies, clinging hasples,

plinges, upright eyeleighs—until she came to a curtained room in the back with a tiny sign reading:

imports

She drew the curtain aside and went in. There were four glass-fronted cages, each with a creature inside. Clockwise from top left, they were labeled:

1. Cochlique: NW Ondanee
2. Terra Huzzi: Outer Terbolontz
3. Lesser Wheek: New Grunb
4. Dog: Oppabof

Pauline knelt down and tapped on the glass. The little dog, a mutt with a heavy preponderance of bull terrier, came to life. It ran in circles and began barking.

"Shh! Shh!"

It wore a collar and a little tag, but Pauline could not read it, the dog was jumping around so much. It was not immediately clear how to open the cage.

A Vyrndeet in a white lab coat appeared.

Pauline immediately said, "I want to buy the dog."

"Really," said the Vyrndeet, crossing its spindly arms. "That'll be fifteen thousand clahd."

"Can I hold him, to make sure I want him?"

"No."

"What's his name?"

"He has no name."

"How did he get here?"

"You have a lot of questions."

"If I'm going to spend fifteen thousand clahd, I'm going to ask questions, and I'm going to get answers."

"You don't look like you have fifteen thousand clahd."

"I am a public prosecutor, and frankly, you don't look like you are in compliance with Donbaloh Civil Practice and Remedies Code Title 5 Section 228.007.(8)(R), which states that all creatures for retail sale must be provided with food and water. I see none in the dog's cage. In fact, I see none in any of these animals' cages. The fine for the first infraction is five thousand clahd. That's four infractions. I saw two Balliopes just outside. Shall I summon them?" Pauline raised her eyebrows.

"No! Please! What do you want?"

"Give me the dog."

"*Give* you the dog?"

"You'll get your fifteen thousand clahd."

The Vyrndeet walked behind the bank of cages and removed the little dog. It ran over to Pauline and went berserk. She knelt down and read its tag.

"I'm Eton.

My master's number is:

(248) 434-5508."

Later she would contact Mersey and have her google the number.

"C'mon, Eton. Let's go get some new shoes."

"Here," said the Vyrndeet, handing Pauline a business card as she left with Eton. "So you know where to send my money."

"Where's the nearest shoe store?"

"Three blocks south, Geep's Footnote."

"Thank you."

"You swindled me, didn't you, human?"

"Wait and see."

Pauline didn't have any sort of leash and was a little worried Eton would run off, but he seemed well trained and stayed right at her heel.

At Geep's, Pauline was immediately hollered at for bringing a pet in the store, so she was forced to leave Eton next to a bollard outside the shop.

"Now, Eton. I'll just be a minute. No chasing charls or Harrow-Teaguers. Hear?"

Eton sat and appeared to grin.

Inside she asked for socks and Euvyd sandals. They came to eighty-eight clahd and were quite comfortable. She raced outside and was relieved to find Eton where she'd left him. They headed back to the connecting jitney in Ohf-dey-Lootn, Pauline boarding with Eton in her arms, and they were soon on their way.

Pauline knocked on the door at 568.145 Jaulareo Bulster and waited. She regarded the door, a study in opulence—jewels and mother-of-pearl, gold and platinum filigree, inlays of . . . rubber? The door suddenly opened, and a female Ult Thivish in a white kimono-like garment stood before her, two charls in her arms, two at her feet. Eton launched himself at the ones on the floor. They separated, confusing the little dog for a moment, until he chose one to go after, but by then it was too late—both were safely in "trees," complex structures covered in carpet remnants built for the amusement of charls and their owners, whose upper reaches were inaccessible to canines and their brethren. Eton turned and looked at Pauline for help and commiseration, but Pauline was awash in embarrassment.

"I'm so sorry," she said. "I wasn't—"

"Who are you?" said Fiolepta Plariant, looking none too patient.

"Pauline Jeopard. I come on urgent business."

"I have never had a human in my flat before," said Fiolepta. "I suppose there is a first time for everything. Come on in."

"Eton!"

"Let him be. He can't hurt the charls; they are far too wily. Now, some welft tea?"

"Er, yes. Please. Thank you."

"Now. How in the world did you get into Donbaloh?"

Pauline told Fiolepta everything.

"And since Tylotch is so hard to find," continued Pauline, "it occurred to me that if anyone had access to him, it would be his mother. And that is why I am here."

"But what do you think Tylotch can do to prevent the miner from breaching the sky?"

"I don't know, but if anyone knows, it will be Tylotch. That's why we need to find him and talk to him. If nothing else, then he needs to order an evacuation. Will you call him?"

"I will do better than that."

"What do you mean?"

"I will have him to dinner. Tonight. And you will be the guest of honor."

CHAPTER 17

A creature Chance had seen only in the halls of Saint Philomene's, a Femma-Thladrook, answered the door, holding the biggest cell phone Chance had ever seen. Darly de Phanxaire was a chimera of a panther's hindquarters and the head and torso of a huge chameleon; she was nine feet long at least and looked as powerful as a tribe of bonobos.

"Yes?"

"I need to see Tylotch Plariant. It's a matter of realm security."

"And you are?"

Chance explained his business as concisely as possible.

Darly de Phanxaire favored him with no expression whatsoever. But that may have just been a property of her species—expressionlessness.

"So," said Chance, peering over her shoulder into the room, "any way I could chat with him for a minute?"

"He's not here."

"I heard you talking to him a few minutes ago. I went to a great deal of trouble to track him down. I know he's in there."

"I don't know what business you had listening at my door, but what you heard," said Darly, holding up her giant cell phone, "was Prefect Plariant on speaker. He's not here. Would you like to come in and look?"

Chance couldn't help himself; he slumped in defeat. Then he straightened up again.

"Can I talk to him on the phone, then?"

"Your story is not independently verifiable."

"You'd rather wait to see blue Oppaboffian sky open up above you and feel the poison of nitrogen-rich air fill your lungs? Those excavators are digging a hundred feet a day through four hundred feet of rock, so we have four days to do something, and I can do nothing on my own. I have people in Oppabof working on the issue, but we are largely powerless. Tylotch alone has the power and authority."

"I repeat: Your story is not independently verifiable."

"What harm is there in letting me talk to him?"

"We're finished here."

 **138**

Darly de Phanxaire shut the door on Chance.

He wasted no time, moving to the next room and placing his glass against the door. Nothing. The next door, nothing, the next door, nothing. The next door:

". . . Glearf Railroad and a thousand clahd for your two utilities and Get Out of Jail Free card."

"No way, *five* thousand clahd, and I keep the Get Out of Jail Free card."

"In your dreams . . ."

Unbelievable: two creatures bickering over a Donbalese version of Monopoly. No time to lose, Chance darted to the next door, room 003.123.

Through his glass, he heard Darly's voice:

". . . thought you should know."

And Tylotch's:

"A human, say you?"

"Yes."

Clearly they were on the phone again, Darly on speaker this time. Chance wasted no time. He banged on the door.

"Prefect Plariant!"

No answer. He placed the glass on the door.

"Tylotch?" Darly implored. "Tylotch?"

"Quiet!" hissed Tylotch. "He's right outside!"

"I can hear both of you, Plariant!" shouted Chance. "Open the door! It's a matter of realm security!"

"Remember your first job with me, Phanxaire?" Chance could hear Plariant whispering. "Remember?"

"Yessir."

"What was it?"

"Bodyguard."

"It is time for you to reactivate that role, spirit yourself to Room 003.123, and absent this human from my proximity."

Down the hall Darly's door burst open, and all at once she was bounding toward him at a terrifying speed with what appeared to be . . . a *bedspread* in her claws. Before Chance could react, she was upon him, draping him head to toe. He soon found himself in a bear hug, upside down, his arms trapped at his sides, cocooned in an institutional bedspread.

"Tylotch!" shouted Darly. "Put down the phone! Run! Now! Safe House 8051680-456! I'll meet you there!"

Chance could hear footsteps, the clomping, stomping footsteps of a large Ult Thivish in motion. The *blenk* of the elevator chime. The doors sliding open, closed. Then Chance's head bumping rhythmically against something . . . oh, Darly's knees; she was walking him somewhere. He felt himself being lifted up, then forced into a small, rectangular space. And he was in motion, downward, fast, faster, then he was in a soft, cool pile. Chance untangled himself.

The laundry hamper. Back where he started.

Now what?

It's sort of comfortable here, in the hamper, thought Chance. *Not terrible at all. And I'm so tired. Sure could use a rest . . .*

Just as Chance was snuggling in for a nap, he remembered that he didn't know where his sister was, and eleven million lives were at stake. He roused himself, sat up straight, and forced himself to think.

Time for a personal State of the Union. What did he know? He had lost Tylotch, and probably Darly; Chance did not know where Safe House 8051680-456 was or how to find it. Even if he did, it was unlikely the prefect would talk to him; his story was not plausible. In Darly de Phanxaire's and Tylotch Plariant's eyes, Chance Jeopard was a nutjob, a fringe citizen, a conspiracy theorist. Reducing his credibility further was his status as a human boy. Moreover, he had lost his sister and his means of contacting her. Logic dictated calling Braig; that's who Pauline would surely contact while waiting to hear from Chance. But Chance had no money and phone calls cost ten clahd. Maybe Braig would accept a collect call? He could try that.

Chance climbed out of the hamper and went to find a pay phone.

CHAPTER 18

 auline?

Mersey, thank heavens, I miss you. What's happening in Oppabof?

Mersey told Pauline everything—about her trip to Rincón Oscuro, about Carver Hebert, about the vitamin B6 capsule with its telepathic cargo.

So we're waiting for Carver Hebert to call you?

Should be any time now. Where are you?

I'm in Tylotch Plariant's mother's personal spa. Three masseuses are currently massaging my hands, feet, and scalp. I think I'm in for acupuncture and cupping. She says it's all to relax me for my audience with Tylotch, who is, evidently, a crazymaker. This is intelligence coming from his mother, now, and is therefore most likely reliable. Oh, and I got a dog. The number on his tag is (248) 434-5508. Here she comes, better go.

Wait, a dog . . . ?

Signing off.

"Pauline, darling," said Fiolepta, who had transformed from her ordinary glamorous self into a supernaturally elegant hostess, though she looked rather piqued. "Tylotch is on his way. I didn't tell him you would be here. He bears a natural mistrust of humans, an instinctual suspicion of disaster theorists, and a reflexive skepticism of youth, so you've got three strikes against you. As such, I think we'd best take precaution."

"Precaution?"

"Please follow Hugulah."

One of the masseuses, a slender Vyrndeet with Wreauvian features, suddenly rose and headed for a small, bright yellow door at the far end of the spa. She opened the door, ducked in, turned, stuck her head back through, and summoned Pauline.

"Come, young human."

Pauline looked around for Eton, who was lying quietly under a love seat in a corner.

"Eton! Come!"

The little dog darted out from under the furniture, and together he and Pauline went through the yellow door into

a vast hexagonal room with a high, vaulted ceiling, everything painted milk white, except the floor, which was carbon black. Five walls were lined with closets. In the center of the room were two freestanding mirrors and a vanity.

Hugulah disappeared the way she had come and closed the door behind her. Pauline was alone with Eton, who was busy sniffing the closets. Strange music commenced. It reminded Pauline of Bo Diddley, but with a Daft Punk feel. She felt like dancing, so she did. This relaxation business was *all right*.

Pauline cut shuffle patterns all over the black floor. The music accelerated, and so did she. She felt gloriously out of control. Eton ignored her, busy with his closet-sniffing enterprise.

The music stopped. A large Fylaria-Lit walked in before Pauline could cease her movement.

"Stop that," it said. "It's time for your transformation."

"Wha?"

"Your transmogrification," said the Fylaria-Lit, who was dressed in black, like Johnny Cash. "That is to say, your conversion, shift, makeover, metamorphosis, about-face, presto-change-o, reformation, metanoia, flip-flop—"

"Okay," Pauline said, out of breath from frantic dancing. "Why?"

"Didn't Madame Plariant explain? The prefect is not likely to tolerate you in your present form. So. I am going to, er, *remodel* you. So you are more presentable. I am, by the

way, Yelvert Etchglinde, chief undertaker to the Prefecture of Donbaloh."

"Undertaker!"

"I am quite good with paints and powders and wigs. We are going to make you look like a Dandelict, an inoffensive species skilled in the conversational arts."

"But the whole point is that I am a human with critical news from Oppabof!"

"I'm sure you will figure something out. Come. Sit at the vanity."

Eton began to bark.

"Oh dear, does that stop?" asked Yelvert.

"I'm going to remain a human and state my case as one."

"That's not going to work for anyone concerned. Please sit."

Pauline sat.

"First let's use a little putty and reshape your nose . . . jus-s-s-s-t so. Good."

Pauline could now *see* the end of her nose. It was sharp as an arrowhead.

"Next let's pop in some yellow contact lenses with central seven-pointed stars . . . open wide . . . good!"

Pauline blinked until the lenses settled comfortably on her corneas. Her vision did not seem much compromised, though it felt like someone had drawn a curtain—everything was a candlepower or two darker.

"Now your chin and forehead . . . these prostheses I

shall adhere by means of a brand of local bubble gum, the best adhesive, I assure you. Just pop a stick in your mouth and chew a moment, good human. . . ."

Sugarless, gross, and highly gummy—it stuck to her fillings with every chomp. Finally Yelvert deemed it ready, and Pauline spit it into his hand. He tore it in two and spread a half onto each prosthetic, then stuck them in place. With a kind of spackle he filled in the gaps.

"Good. Now let's get a little reddish-yellow base down, cover everything up. The-e-e-ere."

The Donbalese's fingertips felt like the erasers on the ends of number two pencils as it worked the makeup into her face and neck, hiding the seams of the prosthetics.

"Now finishing touches, a little eyeliner and some black lipstick."

Mersey would appreciate this, thought Pauline.

"A wig of course. Sit still."

It was a wig like none Pauline had ever seen. Perhaps thirty strands of "hair" flowed from its scalp, each as thick as a finger and falling two feet in a lazy helix. The wig weighed fifteen pounds if an ounce and felt like a diving helmet on her head.

"Have a look, human."

Pauline turned to look in the vanity's mirror. She saw a strange species there and turned away before realizing the species was her. She stared, astonished.

"Now we must dress you. All you need is a navy cloak with a white collar—Dandelicts are very simple dressers."

Yelvert opened a closet and withdrew a beautiful cloak of a strange material. He helped Pauline put it on. She felt like she was a character somewhere between a French nun and Oscar Wilde. It was at least warm; she had cooled off after her dancing and gotten a little chill in the big room.

"I think we are finished here. The prefect will be here soon."

Yelvert knocked on the door, and Hugulah appeared.

"Where's the human?" she said.

"Here," said Pauline. Hugulah covered her mouth and began to titter, genuinely surprised and pleased.

"Come," she said. "Madame Plariant is at table."

Pauline and Eton followed Hugulah out of the hexagon room, through the spa, down a long corridor, through what appeared to be a garage with strange automobiles and air-craft, through an industrial kitchen bustling with creatures stirring pots and deglazing saucepans and slicing vegetables, down another hall, this lined with ancient, regal portraits in gilt frames, and finally into a brightly lit room with several Wreaux in butlers' tails standing around, and Fiolepta Plariant sitting on a green tasseled cushion on the floor. Evidently this was how they were to dine: on the floor.

"Pauline! And Eton. Please join us round the table. Perch yourselves on the violet hassock here next to me.

Eton won't eat the fare, will he? Won't go snuffling about the table like a common Erig-Babst?"

"I don't know. He's new. I found him in a pet store and sort of fooled the owner into giving him to me so I could return him to his owner in Oppabof when I go home."

"I see."

"If I go home."

All at once the magnitude of where she was, what she was doing, and why she was doing it descended upon Pauline like night. A despairing homesickness rose up in her esophagus, and tears squeezed out along her lower lids, threatening to ruin her makeup. Eton noticed, whimpered once, and hid under a flap of her cloak.

It was at that moment that a large door at the far end of the dining room flew open, and in strode a creature clearly related to Fiolepta Plariant. It looked to be in a bad mood.

"Traffic was terrible, Mommy," it said, tossing a hat onto a hat rack. "Donbaloh will never solve the crosstown issue, and no one will tolerate another loop."

"I don't see why you don't just allow air traffic, Tylotch," said Fiolepta. "Like they have at Middlespace in Saint Philomene's. All those jelsairs . . ."

"Jelsairs? Unregulated in the wide-open airspace of Donbaloh? Havoc! Havoc, I tell you! I will never allow it. Creatures can ride in one of the sixteen registered tourist balloons if they want, but that's it."

"Have it your way. Oh, have you met our guest, er, Jeopardine Paulus?"

"Hrmmph," said Tylotch, flopping down on a chartreuse pillow across the floor from Pauline. "How do you do?"

"Hello."

"What's for dinner, Mommy? I hope you didn't have me out here for something yucky, like mantle rat sandwiches or flenth-on-the-cob."

"We're having standard Dojimobi cutlets with hadulous reduction butter and Vlaander beans."

Tylotch groaned.

"It'll have to do."

He clapped, sharply, twice. Attendants in colorful shawls began serving the three diners. One poured a hot, yellowish fluid in a gold-and-crystal goblet; another offered a white napkin folded in the shape of a star; another served a plate with a domed hood. Under the hood was a kind of dinner roll, but black as charcoal and light as a soap bubble. Pauline bit into it. It tasted like a meringue Triscuit, totally edible.

"So, Jeopardine," said Tylotch, "I suppose you have some pressing Dandelictine issue for which you wish to lobby? Now is your chance."

"Actually, sir—"

"Here we go."

"Hear her out, Tylotch."

"What, has she already told you, Mommy?"

"Yes, as a matter of fact."

"Sir," said Pauline, "as you well know, Dandelicts are highly sensitive to atmospheric and seismic vibrations—"

"I did not know that."

"Oh yes, well documented. I am particularly sensitive to the seismic variety, and I have worked with both Dr. Genga Filemangtz at the Donbaloh Geological Society and Professor Horlew Y. U. Dwern at the Department of Volcanic Activity and Predictive Seism, where they employed me principally as a detector."

"A detector. Excuse me, what have you got there in your cloak?"

Pauline lifted the edge of her cloak and liberated Eton, who jumped in her lap.

"Just a dog."

"A dog. *Canis lupus familiaris.* How fascinating."

Tylotch acquired a strange look, one Pauline did not like but which she could not identify.

"Yes. Well. Yesterday I had a day off from my job as a, er, pet store clerk and decided to take a ride in one of the tourist balloons. We traveled very near the ceiling. As we got closer, I sensed a very distinct vibration. An arhythmic vibration coming through the stone of the ceiling. I asked the balloon operator to get as close to the ceiling as possible, to touch the balloon to the rock if he could. That way I could feel the vibrations coming through the fabric of the balloon and down through the ropes securing it to the basket. He

did so. I closed my eyes and 'listened' for a good ten minutes to the vibrations, and I was able to get a good picture of what is happening. I feel that what is most certainly occurring is that there are four large machines digging, at a fairly rapid pace, directly to Donbaloh. I predict they will break through in a matter of days. Of course, this means death for each and every creature in Donbaloh, including you, me, and your mother."

Fiolepta Plariant smiled pleasantly and placed a vast forkful of Dojimobi filet in her mouth.

Tylotch stared menacingly at Pauline.

"I think you are a charlatan, like all the Dandelicts I have known."

Pauline tried to keep her cool.

"You should at least look into it, Plariant. Send a team of seismologists with the proper equipment up to the ceiling, check out my story. What have you got to lose? I mean really."

She gave the prefect of the realm her most dismissive eye roll.

"Mommy," said Tylotch, "I cannot eat this Dojimobi trash, nor these beans. I am starving. I am angry."

Pauline sat quietly, dejected. Incredibly, she had failed. Her ruse, as clever as it had been, had not convinced him. He was going to let Donbaloh perish.

"Jeopardine, my dear," said Tylotch, "I will make a deal with you. I will send a team of mizologists—"

"Seismologists."

"Whatever—up to the ceiling, if you give me your dog."

"You want . . . Eton?"

"If that is his name, then yes, I want Eton."

"What for?"

"I like dogs."

Pauline's mind raced.

"When you verify what I have told you, what will you do to protect Donbaloh?"

"I dunno."

"Can you evacuate?"

"I guess."

"How fast?"

"About three weeks."

"That's not nearly quick enough! You will have to do something to protect the realm."

"I'll talk to the Corps of Engineers. Happy? Now give me the dog."

An attendant picked Eton up out of Pauline's lap.

"Hey!"

The attendant, Eton under her arm, walked over to Tylotch and leaned over so he could whisper in her ear. Pauline only heard the words *spit* and *dressed*. She puzzled over what these might mean. The attendant then left with her dog.

"Good Eton!" shouted Tylotch, then laughed himself almost sick.

Pauline looked over at Fiolepta, who winked at her. What did *that* mean?

"Look, Plariant, you got your new pet, so why not at least make a call or something? Get the balloon launched with the scientists? There's really no time to lose. Do you understand that?"

"All in good time. You might not know this about me—I can't expect that you would—but I don't do anything on an empty stomach. Dinner's going to be a while, so why don't we all sit back and relax."

"Dinner? Aren't we having dinner?"

"Maybe you are. I'm still waiting."

Pauline froze.

Good Eton, Tylotch had said, and laughed.

Good eatin'.

The spit—he was going to roast Eton on a spit!

Pauline tried to remain cool and calm. She waited fifteen seconds and said, as evenly as she could, "May I please use your facilities?"

"Out that door, my dear, down the hall to the right," said Fiolepta.

Pauline waited just outside the door for an attendant to emerge. She followed her as she made her way down a series of corridors to the kitchen. Pauline peeked in the circular window of the double doors leading to the kitchen. There, in a plastic cylindrical cage perched on a stainless steel counter, was Eton. Next to him a Vyrndeet in a tall

white toque was stropping a fourteen-inch knife on a long strip of leather.

Mersey, I need you!

Pauline felt at her throat for her fulgurite necklace. She realized with horror it was not there. Yelvert must have taken it off to apply makeup.

CHAPTER 19

Mersey was in her room at home on her laptop reading about gold mines when her phone rang. It was not a number she knew.

"Miss Marsh, Carver Hebert."

"Hi, any luck?"

"Well, I got the B6 capsule loaded with fulgurite and put it in his vitamin bottle. It only has about eight capsules left, including the special capsule, so he'll take them all before he'd open a new bottle, I'm pretty sure. And that'll happen anytime now."

"All right, thank you. Have you talked with him?"

"No, ma'am. I think he's avoiding me."

"That means we've gotten to him. Good."

"Have you heard from your people down below?"

"No word from Chance, but Pauline is meeting with the guy in charge. She found a dog somewhere."

Mersey had googled the number on Pauline's dog's tag, and it was a mutt named Eton that belonged to a certain Jessy M'bele of Austin. Eton had gone missing earlier in the summer. He was microchipped, but the signal had stopped, a very rare occurrence.

"I wonder how it got there."

"Weird, huh. Would you keep working on Valentine?"

"Will do."

Carver hung up, and Mersey closed her eyes and tried to communicate with Pauline.

We're about ready. Prepare to hear Valentine Sleaford's thoughts in your head at any moment. Pauline?

No response.

If only I was famous.

Mersey perked her head up—a new voice in her head. It had a strange resonance, like a steel guitar in a country blues song.

If I was famous, the voice declared, *Tylotch and Fiolepta wouldn't treat me like a cipher. I would have power, money . . . ohh how I wish I was famous, like Lylameer fe Kopczer or Rhondo Okxscix. They have everything . . . friends, influence, they get the best table at Werfindu's. . . .*

Good day, telepathed Mersey, *I am visiting your brain for a few moments. What is your name?*

Guhhh! Who are you? What are you doing in my head?

Never mind that. Where did you find the fulgurite? The small, tubular mineral you have in your possession?

How could you possibly know that?

Did you take it from Pauline, the human girl, or Chance, the human boy?

Er, Pauline. I took it from her. I'm sorry. It looks nice with my sweater.

Go give it back.

Well, I can't; she's eating. With the prefect. Can't interrupt, no, no. Now, how do I turn you off?

You can't. In fact, I will grow ever more annoying until you restore the fulgurite to Pauline. Would like to hear some poetry I wrote? It's about boys. Listen:

Nooo! Wait! No poetry. I'll return the little doodad. But I have to wait till after their dinner.

CHAPTER 20

The Mingledari Skybond was one of hundreds of very tall, slender buildings in a part of Donbaloh called the Churlish Zone, essentially the financial district, an older section of the realm composed of very narrow, winding streets lined with the offices and storefronts of accountants and procurators, attorneys and comptrollers, statisticians and soothsayers, loan sharks and computer whizzes. There was nary a phone booth to be seen.

Finally Chance approached a young Wreau sitting on a bench doing something with his phone.

"Sorry to bother you—I have to make an emergency call and I lost my phone. May I use yours? I'll be quick."

The Wreau, which looked alarmed at being accosted by a stranger, perhaps especially by a human, shrank away. But nevertheless it offered up its phone.

"Thank you."

Chance stepped away for a little privacy, dialed the operator.

"Calling Braig Toop. I don't have the number. I want to reverse the charges."

Chance held his breath, waiting for his old nemesis, the operator, to recognize him. But apparently a different creature was at the switchboards today.

"You have reached Braig's voice mail; please leave a message."

Curses!

"What's your number?" Chance called to the Wreau on the bench.

"Er, 087 485 7136."

"Braig, Chance. I lost my fulgurite and my sister. I am in the Churlish Zone. Call me at 087 485 7136."

Chance handed the Wreau back its phone and sat down.

"My friend might call, so I'm going to sit and wait with you for a moment, okay?"

"Uh, okay."

"I'm from Oppabof. I'm lost. What do you do?"

"I do school?"

"Oh. Is school out or something?"

"It's summer."

"Oh. It's summer in Oppabof, too."

"Cool. Dude, are those real?"

"What?"

"Your shoes."

"What do you mean?"

"That looks like real rubber."

"Yeah, I guess."

"Don't you know that rubber is like the most valuable thing in Donbaloh? Worth much more than anything else. You're lucky somebody hasn't knocked you over the head and taken those."

"Really?"

"For real."

"How much would you say my shoes are worth?"

"Can I see one?"

Chance handed him a shoe.

"The whole sole and the edges are solid rubber, and it's fairly heavy. I'd say a minimum of thirty thousand clahd. Dude, you should buy yourself some sandals and hide these. I think the only reason no one has noticed is because they're red and not black."

"How do you know so much about rubber?"

"My dad is a horticulturist. He runs the only arboretum in Donbaloh that cultivates rubber trees. There are just six

160

examples in all of Donbaloh. Most rubber is smuggled illegally from Oppabof."

"Where could I sell them?"

"Here in the Churlish Zone. See that store down the road, next to the barbershop, called Zigueloc? They'll pay cash for rubber, though only about sixty percent of market value. It's like a pawnshop."

"Want to make a couple bucks?"

"What?" said the Wreau, looking guarded.

"Let me rephrase. Want to make a thousand clahd?"

"Sure!"

"All you have to do is wait here and take a message if my friend calls. I'll be back."

Chance wasted no time running down to Zigueloc's. He rang the buzzer. After a few moments a panel in the door slid open, and two yellow eyes peered out at him.

"Business?"

"Trade in rubber," said Chance.

The door opened with a loud *tzrzt*. Chance walked inside.

A diminutive Geckasoft sat behind a glass counter with its arms crossed. There was no sign of the yellow-eyed beast that had attended the door, but it was surely not far, watching the proceedings.

"Your business, human?"

"I'd like to sell—"

"Your shoes."

"Yes."

"Let's have a look."

Chance thought it prudent to just hand over one of them.

"I see you don't trust an old Geckasoft. Not many do."

"You're wrong. One of my good friends is a Geckasoft. Yryssy Ayopy. Know her?"

"I know the Ayopy clan by reputation, a bit snobby."

"She's a fine chess player, not to mention a hero. She saved Saint Philomene's Infirmary from a madman."

"Oh. Her. I heard it differently, but all right. I'll give you eight thousand clahd for the pair."

"I understood they were worth quite a lot more."

"It's black rubber that's valuable. Rubber strengthened with carbon black. This dyed stuff has value, but it's been compromised."

Chance suddenly remembered something.

"Just for argument's sake, what would the shoes be worth if they were black rubber?"

"I would estimate forty thousand clahd for the pair. How would you like your funds?"

"One-thousand-clahd notes," Chance said, handing over the other shoe.

"Very well."

"What are your hours today?"

"We are open all the time. Tell me, human: Do you have a source for better-quality Oppaboffian rubber?"

Chance just smiled, shoeless, and took his leave.

When he got back to the bench, the young Wreau was gone. Chance looked around, but the creature was nowhere to be found. Chance happened to look beneath the bench, where he spied a wrinkled plastic bag. Inside was the phone, a worn map, a pair of ragged shoes much like old Keds, and a note, which read:

> Your friend called. As it so happened it was my Uncle Braig. I did not tell you that I am a runaway. It is not summer here in Donbaloh; we do not have summer; school runs all year round. I told Uncle Braig that I am fine, not to worry about me, but I am sure that he called the authorities anyway, so I have moved on. I hope you had luck selling your shoes. I have left you mine to wear; I noticed we were about the same size. I have also left you my trusty Donbaloh map. Oh, the Balliopes will have traced my call and should be appearing any moment. Good luck.
>
> Tracht Roobt

Chance looked up. No Balliopes in evidence yet, but he wasn't taking any chances. He picked up, slipped into the shoes, and ran down a side street, where, incredibly, he found a pay phone. After spending an hour trying to find someone to change a one-thousand-clahd note, he called Braig.

"I can't believe you ran into Tracht. How did he look?"

"Well. He seemed in good shape, good spirits."

"Good. We've been worried about him. And you?"

"I'm fine. Worried about Pauline."

"She's fine. I don't know where she is, but she said she will check in periodically."

"I found Tylotch, but he wouldn't see me."

"You found him! I can't believe how resourceful you humans are."

"I even kind of know where he is now—Safe House 8051680-456. It's in the Bolinjie'Yound District, if that helps."

"Maybe. I'll look into it."

"Braig, do you think Tylotch would accept a bribe?"

"His mother is wealthy, but she keeps a tight rein on the finances. The salary of a prefect is not great, everyone knows. I think, yes, he is ripe for a bribe. It would have to be substantive, though."

"Will you meet me at Zigueloc's on Kiznelpaznel Row in the Churlish Zone in three hours?"

"Zigueloc? That old bum? If you have something to sell, I know a better place, Chance. Go to Dr. Mophiliorp's. It's four doors down and across from Zigueloc's."

"Thanks, I will."

Chance backtracked, passing the bench where he met Tracht, which was now aswarm with Balliopes. He found the Ivrardus Lodge, made his way to the basement, located

the laundry hamper under the chute he'd shot out of, removed the big bedspread Darly de Phanxaire had swaddled him in, and folded it up. Outside he carefully examined the map Tracht had left for him.

Chance plotted his course.

CHAPTER 21

Pauline burst into the kitchen.

"Guys!" she yelled. "I just saw Sasquatch in the hall! He's on his way for an audience with the prefect! C'mon!"

Everyone in the kitchen dropped their eggbeaters and rolling pins and boning knives and ran out into the hallway.

"Thataway! Hurry! Follow the odor!"

Everyone ran off in the direction Pauline pointed. She ducked into the kitchen, which was vacant.

Except for the toque-wearing Vyrndeet stropping the big knife, clearly the head chef. Evidently the appearance of Sasquatch miles below the surface of the Earth was not exciting enough for the chef to abandon her bloodthirsty plans to prepare Eton for spit-roasting.

"Excuse me," said Pauline. "I've just come from the dining room? Prefect Plariant has changed his mind about having dog for dinner."

The head chef did not turn around, nor did she pause in her stropping of the big knife. By now Eton had spied Pauline and was turning in tight, frantic little circles inside his enclosure.

"Miss Chef? Prefect Plariant said he would prefer, uh, macaroni and cheese."

The Vyrndeet stopped stropping. She slowly turned. She stared at Pauline with a red fury the likes of which she had never before witnessed. It was like having the Death Star point its superlaser at her head.

"What," said the head chef, in an incompatibly shrill voice, "is macaroni and cheese?"

"It's an Oppaboffian specialty. Like dog. Only, er, dog-free."

"We don't have any Oppaboffian imports at the moment. Except dog. And dog is what we're having, unless I get orders to the contrary directly from Madame Plariant, Miss de Phanxaire, or the prefect himself. Not some strange, itinerant Dandelict like yourself. What are you doing here, anyway?"

Pauline edged a bit closer. The longer she could keep the Vyrndeet talking, the more time she could buy to try to save Eton.

"Oh, I had dinner with the Plariants. To tell them about the imminent destruction of Donbaloh. Haven't you heard? Everyone's evacuating."

The head chef rolled her eyes, returned to her stropping. That knife was going to be supernaturally sharp. "Okay, little dog, let's see what you're made of."

"Wait! Can I take a quick look at it?"

"If you must."

Creatures were slowly filing back into the kitchen, crestfallen looks on their faces.

"No Sasquatch," they muttered. "Elusive as ever."

"Say," said Pauline, addressing the head chef, "can you make something taste like dog?"

"I can make hydrated silica taste like delecta makindee," she said, puffing up.

"Really?" said Pauline. "Well, I have a culinary challenge for you. The prefect is expecting dog, but this particular beast is a poisonous breed known as *muttus domesticus venomus*, and anyone who tastes its flesh will perish in writhing agony. But as we all know, the prefect cannot be disappointed; he is expecting dog. So, if you can send a convincingly doggy dish to table, in secrecy, peace will reign."

The head chef beamed her furious superlaser at Pauline again.

"How do you know it's poison?"

"I work in a pet store. I'm an expert in Oppaboffian exports, especially dogs. You can test me if you like."

Pauline closed her eyes, as if expecting a quiz. She could feel the head chef's burning glare.

"If I am caught," said the Vyrndeet, "I could be fired and sent to the commissary kitchen at the pumice mines, my heavens."

"Yes, but if you succeed, it will be one of your greatest gastronomic triumphs and something for your memoir."

"Ye-e-e-es," said the head chef, stroking her chin. "Yes. I will do it. Sous-chef! Bring me pearl bignols, higley sauce, and a Popses flank, butterflied! Prepare the coals and spit!"

The kitchen was suddenly in full operation. Pauline wasted no time liberating Eton, who did his berserker thing around her ankles. They withdrew, and she found herself in a rococo hallway, Eton at her ankles, realizing she knew not what to do next. She had no fulgurite, no way of knowing if the prefect would keep his promise, if her ruses would work, if he would be fooled by the "dog" simulacrum dinner of Popses flank, whatever that was. She did not know how to get out of the building, nor where to go if she did. Time was surely running short—Sleaford's excavators were most certainly working 24-7.

Feeling a measure of despair for the first time, Pauline sat down in the hallway and hugged her dog.

CHAPTER 22

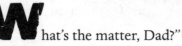hat's the matter, Dad?"

Carver Hebert Jr., or Ti-Cee, as he was known ("Ti" was short for "Petit"), observed his father sitting across from him in the booth at the Mercury Café. Carver Sr. hadn't touched his Triple MercBurger or his fries or his shake and seemed to be staring at an invisible object hovering somewhere between the pie spinner and the rack of free promotional tourist brochures. Ti-Cee snapped his fingers a couple of times.

"Dad?"

"Yes, Son?"

"You're acting a little weird. Staring, fasting, vow of silence. What's up?"

Ti-Cee had his eye on his father's untouched meal. Ti-Cee was fourteen, growing at roughly an inch an hour, and always ravenous. He had once eaten, in a single sitting, an entire box of Scooter Pies, a dozen lemon-lime Italian ices, and a punch bowl of orange Jell-O.

"Nothing to speak of."

"C'mon, Dad. I can tell. Is it the Longhorns?"

"No, no."

"Is it Txscissoropses?"

Txscissoropses was their little tuxedo cat that was always getting into trouble. The Heberts had adopted her from two women who swore the kitten was descended from an Aztec god, and thus named her accordingly. She was indeed imperious and ran the household.

"No, she's been behaving the best she can."

"Is it the Kaleidoscopes?"

Carver Sr. raised orchids, species Phalaenopsis Baldan's Kaleidoscope, as a hobby.

"No, they're looking robust."

"So . . . what, then?"

Carver Sr. was silent for a long moment.

"Watch out," said Ti-Cee, helping himself to his father's fries. "If you don't tell me your problems, I'll tell you mine."

"Well, it's Valentine."

"Oh."

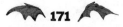

And just like that Carver Sr. opened up to his son. He told him everything. About Donbaloh, the gold, Pauline, Chance, and Mersey. Fulgurites. The eleven million. *The problem.*

"Now this is something of a secret, Son, you hear?"

"I can't believe what you're telling me, Dad. I mean I can, and I do, but I can't. You know?"

"Yes."

"I also can't believe you know Mersey Marsh. She's kind of famous, you know."

Ti-Cee, who volunteered in the theater department at his high school as a makeup artist, often acquired tips from YouTube and frequently encountered Mersey's very popular tutorials.

"And that makes you pretty dang cool," added Ti-Cee.

"This world," said Carver Sr., shaking his head, "it's too small."

"Have you talked to him? Valentine, I mean."

"No, not yet. He wouldn't listen anyway, then he'd fire me."

Ti-Cee was growing tired of Rincón Oscuro. He and his father had dropped everything to move here on this open-ended business trip. Ti-Cee had left his friends back in Beaumont and was aching to see them. As selfish as it was, he actually would not have minded if Valentine let his father go. But what would he do? His father was essentially a bodyguard and handler to a very wealthy and somewhat

demented industrialist well known for his mercenary tactics, invidious strategies, and delusions of world harmony. Stepping down from such a position would look weird on a résumé and might be difficult to parse in a job interview. Ti-Cee did not envy his dad.

An old woman wandered into the Mercury Café and sat two booths down from Carver Sr. and Ti-Cee. She looked tough, weatherworn, like maybe she made her own barbed wire. She ordered a black coffee and a bowl of chili.

"Bring me some Tabasco, too, honey, a crime it ain't already on the table."

"Yes, Mrs. Radegast," said the waitress.

"Dad," whispered Ti-Cee, "is that—"

"How's the operation going out at Little Yucca, Mrs. Radegast?" said Carver Sr.

"Well, it's noisy. I can hear it clear over the hill; the racket sneaks in the house with all the windows shut."

"How far's he dug?"

"Cain't say for sure, two hundred foot? Big ol' hole."

"Now, you're not worried about the possible collapse, I'm guessing."

Ti-Cee looked at his father. What was he up to?

"The collapse?"

The chili and Tabasco arrived, but Frieda Bull Radegast ignored them. To Ti-Cee's annoyance, his father started back in on his Triple MercBurger. After a big bite and a long swallow, he said:

"The collapse. I heard Valentine Sleaford telling an investor on the phone there was a slim to middlin' chance that when they broke through, it would destabilize the area, geologically speaking, and create a sinkhole roughly a mile in diameter."

"A mile across? Would my—"

"Yes, your ranch house would be within the radius."

"How deep—"

"Between ten and twelve miles."

"I see."

"There would be no survivors."

Ti-Cee noticed the waitress standing wide-eyed and openmouthed, a coffee globe in one hand, spilling decaf on the floor.

"Rincón Oscuro is out of the danger zone, right, Dad?"

"That's right," said Carver Sr., seeing the waitress, too. "Too far from the epicenter. You're perfectly safe here in town, dear."

"I see Valentine all the time out at the site," said Frieda. "Isn't he afraid?"

"They're just not close to breaching yet. When they get close, he'll go back to Lubbock."

"What about the people operating the machinery?"

"I guess he won't tell them. He needs them to dig."

"That ain't right."

"He didn't mention the possible collapse to you? It's not in your contract?"

"No it is not," said Frieda Bull Radegast, who had still not touched her chili, or even opened the saltines that came with it.

"Maybe best not to mention it to him. Maybe best to just nullify your contract with him and stop the mining, no questions asked."

"But I need that money, young man."

"Respectfully, I don't know what good that money'll do if you and your homestead are buried beneath a trillion tons of rock and dirt twelve miles below the surface of the Earth. Do you?"

Frieda Bull Radegast opened up the saltines, crumbled them in her fist, and sprinkled them into her chili. She opened another pack and did the same. She drowned her chili in Tabasco, drank down the rest of her coffee and tapped the rim with a gnarled forefinger, indicating her desire for more. While the waitress ran to fetch it, Frieda started in on her chili. She ate it all, then dabbed at her lips with a napkin.

"I don't want to disappear into no sinkhole," said Frieda, sipping at her third refill. "I can get by without the money. I'll tell him to stop."

"That's fine, Mrs. Radegast," said Carver Sr. "Just fine."

CHAPTER 23

Braig's nephew Tracht's map was folded in sixteenths, a well-worn thing that illustrated streets, waterways, famous buildings, jitney lines, subways, bus routes, and even areas tourists should avoid.

Chance had noticed that some Donbalese rode around in wheeled carriages much like rickshaws, driven by a species of creature he had never seen doing anything else, a sort of chimerical dragon/mule thing, compact and muscular.

A rickshaw drove perilously close to Chance, and he nearly dropped the map.

"Hey!"

"Are you hailing me?" shouted the driver, who was clearly having a bad day.

"How much to go here?"

Chance showed the creature a spot on the map in front of the Donbaloh Public Library.

"Thirty-five clahd plus tip. You got that, human?"

"I got it; let's go."

"Humans pay in advance."

Chance gave him a one-hundred-clahd coin, a gold hexagon with a hole in it.

"You can have it all, but you have to wait for me and bring me back here. Okay?"

"You got it, human. Get in, no seat belts, hold on!"

They took off like a one-man Roman chariot through the crowded streets.

"What are you?" shouted Chance. "What kind of creature?"

"Recaphrey," said the Recaphrey. "Name's Oolt-Dod."

"Are all your kind rickshaw drivers?"

"Either that or lawyers. I could have been a lawyer, but the rickshaw exam is harder than the bar and I wanted a challenge. Passed the first time. I know every street address in Donbaloh."

"Really? What about Safe House 8051680-456 in the Bolinjie'Yound District?"

The Recaphrey galloped along in silence for a while.

"I don't know it. I daresay it's not a real address, or it's a

 **177**

code name for a place with a genuine street address. What is it?"

Chance decided to take a chance. He explained everything to Oolt-Dod.

"And Safe House 8051680-456 is where Tylotch is holed up, I'm pretty sure. I need to see him. I think I can convince him to listen."

"But how, if he hasn't so far?"

"You'll see. Are we there yet?"

The rickshaw came to a shuddering stop.

"Here."

"I'll be back."

Chance grabbed the bedspread and made his way carefully down to the banks of the Yalphala River. It was dark as a coal miner's basement, and he could barely see. He felt his way along the bank until he came to a thick, old piling holding up a rickety pier. At the foot of the piling was what he came for.

The raft. Made of 100 percent black rubber, at least thirty-five pounds of the stuff. He wrapped it in the bedspread, hoisted it over his shoulder, and climbed up the bank and back to the rickshaw.

"To Dr. Mophiliorp's, on Kiznelpaznel Row."

"I know where that is. What have you got there? A big bunch of black rubber? Haw-haw-haw!"

"Ha-ha-ha!"

The ride back was slower; traffic had thickened. Chance fell asleep.

"Arriving: Dr. Mophiliorp's, Kiznelpaznel Row."

"Will you wait for me?"

"Sure thing."

Braig was not yet in evidence, so Chance entered the shop.

A young Dandelict sat cross-legged on a tall barstool in front of a glass case of costly-looking timepieces. She peered at Chance curiously, without hostility.

"I'm here to see Dr. Mophiliorp."

"I'm Dr. Mophiliorp."

Chance thought he succeeded in hiding his surprise, but Dr. Mophiliorp said:

"Surprised?"

"No, no."

"What have you got for me?"

"Oppaboffian rubber."

"Let's have a look."

Chance unwrapped the bedspread, revealing the rubber raft. It was the Dandelict's turn to show surprise. She leaned forward, touched it.

"May I test it?" she asked.

"Please."

Dr. Mophiliorp produced a small scalpel, two squirt bottles of liquid, and a petri dish. She carefully shaved a sliver

of rubber away, placed it in the dish, and sprayed it with one liquid, then the other. The not-unpleasant, nostalgia-inducing scent of burned rubber began to fill the room.

"Hmm, very good-quality vulcanized rubber. What do you want for it?"

"Clahd."

The Dandelict spent a long time going over every inch of the raft—washing it, removing the non-rubber fixtures like oarlocks—then weighed it.

"I can give you 1.26 megac."

"What's that?"

"One megac is a million clahd."

"Wow. What about, er, taxes?"

"You are responsible for those."

"I'll take it."

Dr. Mophiliorp disappeared behind a curtain with the rubber raft and emerged with a thick envelope. She opened it and removed a stack of small, crisp banknotes no larger than baseball cards. She counted out 126 of them and pushed the stack toward Chance.

"It is good you came to me. Other dealers would have cheated you. Zigueloc, for example, or Beurler."

A little bell chimed, and the door to the shop opened. Braig strode in.

"Doctor, you are treating our human well, I presume?"

"Why, Braig, I thought you were busy with rehearsals for *Verve Clandox*."

"Just taking a few hours off to meet with Tylotch Plariant, and save Donbaloh from ruin."

"Ha-ha-ha!" Dr. Mophiliorp laughed a little like Scooby-Doo. She stopped when she realized neither Chance nor Braig were laughing along with her.

"Why, what's up?" said the doctor.

Chance explained.

"So you might best close up shop and evacuate until the trouble blows over."

Outside, the rickshaw was still waiting. The driver summoned Chance over.

"I've been thinking about your Safe House 8051680-456 conundrum, and I think I have a theory."

"Yes?"

"If one were to think of numbers as letters—8 as *B*, 5 as *S*, 6 as *G*, et cetera, then 8051680 would 'spell' BOSIGBO, which is the name of an apartment building. Guess what district it's in?"

"Bolinjie'Yound!"

"Correct. And 456 would presumably be the apartment number."

"Well done! Will you take me and Braig there now?"

"Climb in! No seat belts! Here we go!"

The rickshaw rocketed through the narrow streets, and Braig and Chance held on for dear life.

"Braig, all this talk of evacuation. Where would everyone go?"

"At the northwest end of Donbaloh is the opening to a sixteen-mile tunnel that leads to another, larger prefecture, Ontagrawnt. There have been evacuations before. Every Donbalese family has an Ontagrawntian family they can stay with. Evacuations are usually orderly affairs, but they take a long time. They can't be accomplished in just a few days. At least they never have before. If Tylotch were to order one, it would take ten days at least to get everyone out. And I think your miner is working faster than that."

"So we have to hope Tylotch has a way of stopping a breach."

"Or that Mersey can stop the miner."

"Or Pauline. I hope she's okay."

"She probably has a plot of her own."

CHAPTER 24

Valentine Sleaford stood in his trailer in his bathrobe with his hands on his hips, staring at the scraps of paper on the floor. Frieda Bull Radegast had just paid him a visit and torn her contract up in front of him and demanded he stop mining on her property, right this minute, that he could keep his money, no explanation.

This was highly irregular, and he would have to run it by his legal team. Valentine of course would not stop digging in the meantime.

He set to frying himself some bacon and eggs. He poured a glass of no-pulp orange juice, went into the bathroom, and took all his daily pills. Vitamin D2, vitamin E, vitamin C, biotin, vitamin K, vitamin B12, and, of course, a nice healthy dose of vitamin B6. He downed everything in one swallow and finished off the orange juice.

He went back in the kitchenette and placed some bread in the toaster. He wondered what the deal was with Mrs. Radegast, if perhaps Mersey Marsh had somehow gotten to her.

I had nothing to do with it, Sleaford.

Valentine stopped everything. He tapped his skull with a fingertip. He shook his head, hard, and resumed cooking.

We're going to be companions for a while, Sleaford. I'm going to be right here in your head.

"Who are you!" Valentine screamed inside his empty trailer. His bacon and eggs were beginning to burn. The toast popped up.

You've met the reasonable Mersey Marsh. Well, now meet the unreasonable Mersey Marsh.

"This is impossible!"

It's not, really. But you can make it stop.

"How! How!"

Call off your excavators. Abandon the project.

"Never!"

Let me put it another way: I will not go away unless you halt the project, for good.

—whimper—

I can get much more annoying than just a voice in your head, believe me. Would you like me to demonstrate?

"Nooo!"

You don't have to talk to communicate, you can just think, Sleaford.

Like this?

Right. Now where were we? You were going to call off the mining project.

Can't do that. Getting close.

Then I am going scream.

No, please—

Eeeeeeeeeeeeeeeeeeeeeeeeeeeeeeeeeeeeeeeeeeeeeeeeee

That was horrible, ple—

Eeeeeeeeeeeeeeeeeeeeeeeeeeeeeeeeeeeeeeeeeeeeeeeeee

Sto-o-o-p!

Eeeeeeeeeeeeeeeeeeeeeeeeeeeeeeeeeeeeeeeeeeeeeeeeee

You win! I'll stop the mining project. Just get out of my head!

How will you prove it to me?

You'll just have to call Frieda Bull Radegast and ask her.

I'm holding you to it, Sleaford.

Greasy smoke filled the trailer. Valentine's toast was cold.

You ruined my breakfast, you know.

No response.

He opened the door, set a box fan on the threshold, and turned it on high. Then he sat on the floor behind the fan

and began to brood. He had faced opposition to his mining operations before. In Nevada there had been the southwestern willow flycatcher, in South Dakota the reservation property line dispute, in California the mineral rights fiasco, in Colorado the water conservation people, in Oregon the Save the Spotted Frog Society. But none of them had used advanced mind-control techniques.

Valentine listened to the rumble and roar of the four Bucyrus RH400 excavators in the distance. It was a kind of discordant symphony. He knew each machine well, their individual voices—there was Clarice, the oldest machine, whose engine raced in hot weather; Simon, who groaned like Sisyphus when climbing hills; Darnold, who purred like a jungle cat under the heaviest loads; and Imp, the newest, who was so quiet her engines resonated only when the others were idle. Together the music they made brought Valentine comfort and peace. He could easily fall asleep to their gnashy din and could just as easily be jarred awake by the cessation of it.

And now he was being forced to stop his machines, forced to give up his dream of an immeasurable gold strike, forced to abandon his effort to fight poverty the only way he knew how. By an impetuous girl who could somehow throw her voice into his head.

Valentine Sleaford slowly stood.

CHAPTER 25

Eton, evidently tired of being hugged so desperately, wriggled away from Pauline and sat a short distance away. He then pricked up his ears, ran down the gilt-and-lapis hallway of the Plariant mansion, turned a corner, and disappeared.

"Eton!"

Pauline was in no mood to go chasing after the dog she'd just saved from consumption. She trusted he would come back.

And he did. He was dragging some creature by the coattails. The creature was wailing, "Halp! Halp!"

"Yelvert!" exclaimed Pauline, standing and rushing toward him. "Eton, let go of him!"

Eton obeyed, and Yelvert was free. He brushed himself off, then said:

"I have something of yours."

"My fulgurite! Thank you, Yelvert."

"I don't want any more of that sorcery in my head. I like to hear my own thoughts, uninterrupted, and that's all. Here."

Pauline donned the necklace.

Mersey?

Oh no, now what? Not Mersey, but a voice in her head she recognized yet had not heard in some time.

Who's this?

Valentine Sleaford, who's this?

Mersey had somehow secreted a fulgurite fragment onto Sleaford's person—miraculous!

Not important. I'm going to direct you to abandon your mining operation or—

You're kind of late to the party, aren't you? Mersey already threatened me. I was just on my way to tell the machine operators to cease and desist.

Really?

Is this Pauline?

Maybe.

It is! Pauline, you and Mersey win. I give up. But you have to get out of my head, now. That's the deal.

 188

Pauline really didn't want to have Valentine Sleaford in her head any more than he wanted her in his, so she took the fulgurite necklace off and tucked it into her sock, where it could do no communicating, then breathed a mighty sigh of relief. It was over. All she had to do now was find her brother and get out of here.

Yelvert was still standing there. He looked like he was awaiting instruction or guidance.

"Yelvert, I need a phone."

"Um. One floor up, end of the hallway."

"Don't they have cell phones in Donbaloh?"

"Just young people, it seems." Yelvert sighed, as though youth were going to take over and there was nothing he could do to stop it.

"Another thing. How do we get out of Donbaloh?"

"Why, I don't know. How did you get in?"

"I don't think I could find it again."

With Eton following close at her heel, Pauline found the staircase to the second floor and eventually a private phone in a small alcove dominated by a marble bust of Tylotch Plariant. Pauline called Braig, but no one answered. Disappointed that she could not speak to him directly, she left a message.

"Braig, Sleaford has agreed to stop mining. All is well. I need to find you and my brother and figure a way out of Donbaloh."

But deep down Pauline knew it wasn't going to be that simple.

She turned around, and there was Yelvert. He had followed her up the stairs.

"Yelvert, is there a department of seismology in Donbaloh?"

"Pull on Tylotch's brooch, there."

On the bust was an ornate brooch, also carved from marble. Pauline took hold of it and pulled. A drawer slid out from the plinth on which the bust rested. Inside the drawer was a phone book. Pauline found a number for the Donbaloh Seismological Society and called it.

"DSS," said an authoritative feminine voice.

"Hi, can you tell me if the Donbaloh Seismological Society can pinpoint Oppaboffian mining activity?"

"Yes. We have sensors all over the Donbalese 'sky,' though they only cycle through one sector at a time."

"I have reason to believe there is a major mining operation above Donbaloh, right now, and it might break through. Can you turn on all of the sensors and locate it?"

"Yes, please stand by."

Unbelievable—Pauline was not being questioned. Thank heaven for scientists.

"Miss? Yes, significant activity is registering over Sector 3gM-8901."

"Where is that?"

"It happens to be directly above the Zekophane-Chthonica."

"The Zek—"

"You're not from around here, are you? The Zekophane-Chthonica is Donbaloh's tallest freestanding building, on the banks of the Yalphala in the Foldnir-Northeast District. The top of the building is only about forty feet below the stone sky. On the roof of the building are a dozen lighted tennis courts and a hot-air balloon concession."

"So if the miner broke through he would find himself on the roof of the Zekophane-Chthonica?"

"Squarely."

"Um, I think it's possible a miner might, in fact, break through. I'm from Oppabof, and I have information about the miner. His goal is to reach Donbaloh. He may have stopped after being persuaded not to break through, but, frankly, I don't trust him."

"That would be devastating, to say the least."

"What can be done?"

"Call me back later, I have to consult with my superiors. The name's Glandaw."

"Pauline."

"Okay, Pauline, we'll figure this out. And thank you. We take threats to the breach of our realm very seriously."

CHAPTER 26

The Bosigbo Apartments were a run-down collection of slender buildings in a dodgy section of the realm located south of the river. Chance patted the stack of ten-thousand-clahd notes in his pocket, climbed out of the rickshaw, and, with Braig at his side, took an elevator to the forty-fifth floor. They listened at the door to Apartment 456.

". . . had roast Oppaboffian dog at Mommy's house, Darly. You should have come."

"I was getting the safe house ready, Tylotch, it was a mess. Besides, I don't like dog, and Fiolepta doesn't like me."

"Mommy doesn't like anybody."

"Really?"

"Well, she *did* seem to like our dinner guest, some little Dandelict girl who wants me to send scientists to the ceiling. I'm not going to, though."

"Who was she?"

"She called herself Jeopardine Paulus."

Pauline! thought Chance.

"Braig, we need a phone, quick!" he whispered.

"I saw one in the lobby."

"You wait here—I'll be right back."

In the lobby of the Bosigbo, Chance dialed information and got a number for Fiolepta Plariant.

"Hello?"

"Hi, I'm trying to get in touch with a visitor of yours, Jeopardine Paulus?"

"I'll page her."

Over the line Chance could hear the page: *Jeopardine Paulus, pick up a house phone and press six for an incoming call. Repeat: Jeopardine Paulus, pick up a house phone and press six for an incoming call.*

And a few moments later, he heard his sister's voice for the first time in what seemed like ages.

"Hello?"

"Pauline, it's me."

"Chance! How—"

"Never mind, I found Plariant."

 **193**

Pauline told her brother everything she knew, including Plariant's promise to send scientists to the stone sky, the Donbaloh Seismological Society, and Sleaford's oath to stop mining.

"I don't trust him, though," said Pauline.

"We need Tylotch to mobilize the Corps of Engineers," said Chance. "Only he can do it. Listen, I sold the rubber raft—"

"Chance, we might need that!"

"I know, but rubber is worth a fortune, and I thought I could bribe Tylotch."

"A good idea, but I don't know. . . ."

"Let's meet at the top of the Zekophane-Chthonica building in one hour, at center court."

"Are we going to play tennis?"

"I guess we have to do something while we're waiting for Sleaford's excavators to poke through."

Chance took the elevator back to the forty-fifth floor, where he found Braig still listening at Tylotch's door.

"I think Darly's taking a shower."

"Braig, do we just knock?"

"We just knock."

They knocked. Tylotch answered the door.

"Not you again. How did you find me?"

"I have an offer for you, Plariant."

Chance took out his folded stack of clahd. Tylotch audibly gasped.

194

"There's 1.2 million here. It's all yours if you notify the Corps of Engineers that an Oppaboffian miner with heavy equipment will break though to Donbaloh directly above the Zekophane-Chthonica building very soon, and give the Corps free rein to deal with the matter as they see fit, since there's no time to evacuate."

"Okay, give it, give it."

"Half now, half after I have seen that you have fulfilled your promise."

"Sure, give."

Chance peeled off sixty 10,000-clahd notes and slapped them in Tylotch's palm.

"Now, call," said Chance.

Tylotch picked up his phone and dialed a number.

"Colonel Tquidlov, Tylotch Plariant here. We seem to have a situation."

Plariant and the colonel talked for a long time. Finally Plariant hung up.

"Done, human. Now when do I get the rest of my money?"

"I'll call you with the location, once I verify the Corps is handling the situation. Let me ask you something, though, Plariant. Why so resistant? Donbaloh is in peril, and you hide."

"You don't know what my life is like. All day I listen to doomsayers telling me Donbaloh is in imminent danger. They're all nuts, like you. You're just more persistent and

resourceful. Whatever fears you have, you'll soon see will prove unfounded."

"C'mon, Braig, let's go."

Their rickshaw driver was waiting for them.

"I figured you guys would be back before long. Where to?"

"The tallest building in Donbaloh."

CHAPTER 27

Yelvert had disappeared, and Pauline realized she had no idea how to exit the Plariant mansion. As she was weighing her options, the phone rang.

"Pauline, Glandaw here. I have spoken with my superiors. Based on information from the sensors, we estimate the miners could break through sometime in the next six to eight hours. The Corps of Engineers has a plan. I will meet you at the Zek-Chthon as soon as you can get there. A human, you say?"

"Yes, but I won't be the only one. My brother will be there, too. What's the plan?"

"Let's just say it involves building. And we can use all the help we can get."

Pauline hung up. She looked around, then headed off down the hall.

"Come, Eton."

Eton bounded after her, tongue flapping wildly.

At the end of the hall a large ornate door stood ajar. Before Pauline could decide whether to enter, Eton had nosed it open and run inside.

A scream.

Pauline ran in to find a small Euvyd standing on a chair, holding her skirts in bunches. Eton was licking her shoes.

"Get it off me, get it off!"

"Eton, come here!"

Eton disobeyed, and Pauline had to pick him up so he would leave the poor Euvyd alone.

"Is that your creature?" The Euvyd remained on the chair.

"Yeah. His name is—"

"What is it?"

"An Oppaboffian dog."

"Will it hurt me?"

"Dogs are nothing but affection and drool."

After a moment the Euvyd climbed down from the chair, snatched a broom from a corner, and wielded it like a staff.

"We'll leave you alone. I just need to know how to get out of this mansion. Can you tell me?"

"Just go down the hall, take a left and then another left, board an elevator to the ground floor, take a right down a long hall, a left at the bronze statue of Tylotch Plariant jousting, then a right at the fountain, and through the doors ahead of you outside and onto Jaulareo Bulster."

Pauline squeezed her eyes shut so she could commit the litany of directions to memory.

"Thank you. Sorry to have startled you."

Pauline turned to leave.

"Wait. Were you Madame Plariant's dinner guest?"

"I was, yes."

"I think they're looking for you. Security did not look happ—"

Pauline ran off, Eton at her ankles, before the maid could finish her sentence.

Out on Jaulareo Bulster, Pauline looked around for a creature whom she could ask for directions, but the street was deserted. She happened to look up in the darkness of Donbaloh and saw a distant building that seemed to climb so high it disappeared into the murk of the firmament. It was by far the tallest structure she could see.

"See that, Eton? Couldn't be more than three miles away. Let's go!"

Pauline and Eton began making their way through the creature-less streets toward the towering building. Soon

they encountered the river and had to walk more than a mile before they found an underpass. It was also deserted, and dark as night. Pauline felt her way along the walls, which were slick, cold, and damp.

Then she bumped into something . . . warm.

"Hello? Who is disturbing my rest?"

Pauline jumped back, and Eton barked.

"Sorry!" she said. "I just can't see."

"Everyone bumps into me."

"Who are you?"

"I am Tym, a Fylaria-Lit from Pangforg Division, a stone's throw from here. I'm a bricklayer by trade. I'm in hiding from my brother, Wym, who is angry at me for cheating in a game of cassalah."

"What is cassalah?" Pauline liked the sound of Tym's voice. It soothed her. She was in a hurry, though—no time to chat. "A card game?"

"Board game. You've not heard of it? Are you not from around here?"

"Oppabof."

"Ah! Of course. I haven't heard a human accent in some time, years even. What is your business here?"

"Long story."

Pauline had a thought. Glandaw had said that the Corps of Engineers would need as much help as they could get, and they were going to be building something. What better builder than a bricklayer?

"I have a lot of long stories myself. Mostly about laying brick. Or cheating at cassalah. I always hide in a tunnel after I get caught."

"Speaking of bricks," said Pauline, "how would you like to help with a municipal, um, project? We might need a bricklayer."

The Fylaria-Lit was quiet for a moment, as though weighing its options.

"Sure, why not? As long as Wym doesn't find me."

"Do you know the fastest way to the Zek-Chthon?

"Are you kidding? I know a tunnel that goes right there. Follow me."

"But I can't see!"

"I brought a flashlight. Ah, here we are."

And then there was illumination. The Fylaria-Lit began loping off, a strange kangaroo-like gait that covered ten feet in a bound.

Eton ran on ahead, his shadow long in the beam of the flashlight, but Pauline had trouble keeping up. They ran through not-so-shallow puddles of slimy water, past encampments of odd, unidentifiable creatures huddled around greasy trash-can fires, and the occasional deeply asleep creature stretched serenely along the edge of the tunnel.

"Turning left!" shouted Tym, then ducked into a much smaller side tunnel that Pauline had to crouch—knees bent, head down—to navigate. The tunnel went on seemingly forever, and her thighs began to burn. Just as she was about

tell Tym to stop, that she had to rest, they emerged in a large, oval room. Tym stopped and shined the flashlight at the walls.

"I bricked this room myself," he said. "Took two weeks, using the best cinder blocks and most durable cement."

"Where are we?" Pauline was almost fatally out of breath.

"Sub-sub-subbasement of the Zek-Chthon. There's a staircase around here that'll take us to the—wait . . ."

Tym shined the flashlight on Pauline for the first time.

"You're . . . you're a Dandelict!"

"No, it's just makeup and a wig. I'm in disguise. It's part of the 'long story.'"

"Dandelicts aren't allowed in the Zek-Chthon. Stems from an incident involving a water balloon and an elevator shaft. You have to get that stuff off you."

Tym stuck the flashlight in a small crevice in the bricks so that it shone down on the two companions and illuminated a section of the vast basement.

"The guy that applied it said all I have to do is get a grip on the wig at the back of my neck and pull upward."

"Really? Let's try it."

Pauline turned around. Tym got a good hold on the wig and lifted. With a nauseating sucking sound, the wig and mask of makeup all peeled off in one piece. Tym stood there with the "head" in one hand, like a French executioner.

"Gross," they said in unison, then started to laugh.

"That cloak is still kind of weird, but not much we can do about that. But you'd better remove the seven-pointed-star contacts."

She had forgotten about the contacts. Pauline took a moment and removed each one. *Ah, that's better.*

Forty-five minutes and four separate elevator rides later, the pair, plus Eton, emerged on the roof of the Zekophane-Chthonica.

A chaotic scene greeted them.

Hundreds of creatures of all stripes running this way and that across the tennis courts, whose nets had been taken down. Dozens more creatures standing on ladders building what appeared to be a barrier out of large cinder blocks around the perimeter of the building. It was already six or seven feet high. Cinder blocks stood in piles everywhere, waiting to be added to the barrier.

"Ah, my people!" said Tym, his hand on his heart.

"Pauline!"

She was smiling even before she turned toward the voice.

"Chance!"

Her brother came running across a tennis court, dodging creatures carrying cinder blocks. Brother and sister fell into a hug.

"I've never been so glad to see you," they said at the same time.

"Are you wearing black lipstick?" Chance said.

Pauline had forgotten about that, too.

"Long story."

"I'll bet."

"And this is Eton," said Pauline, presenting the little dog. Eton was doing his berserker thing again, spinning in tight circles and slobbering like a pug.

"So delighted you're safe and sound, my dear," said Braig.

"Me too. I missed you, Braig."

"And this is . . . ?" said Braig.

"Guys," said Pauline, "meet Tym. He's a bricklayer. I found him in a tunnel."

Braig gave Tym a deep bow, which Tym awkwardly returned.

"Enchantée," said Tym. "Now somebody lead me to the blocks!"

A very lithe and beautiful Wreau approached them. She was wearing overalls and covered in sweat.

"Chance and Pauline, I presume," said the Wreau. "I'm Glandaw, director of the Donbaloh Seismological Society and technical advisor to Project Penthouse."

"This is Braig, and this is Tym, both here to lend a hand."

"There is no time to lose," said Glandaw. "The miners are within a few yards of breaking through. Our goal is to extend the height of the Zek-Chthon so that it meets the stone sky, the ceiling, if you will, forming a vast room—a penthouse—actually a kind of cinder block air lock so our atmospheres don't mix and the air pressure doesn't

destabilize. The barrier is going up at a rate of about four feet an hour, so it'll take about four more hours to complete. It will then require another few minutes to spray it with a sealant. We were low on sealant until this morning, when an unexpected call came from a local pawnbroker who'd acquired a large cache of natural Oppaboffian rubber. She gave it to the DSS as a gift. I can't help but wonder if you humans are part of the chain of provenance."

"It was the raft we used to access Donbaloh," said Pauline.

"Right. Now, Chance, your job is to hand out gas masks. Make sure every creature gets one. Each species must get the mask designed for it. A mask for a Geckasoft will not fit a Harrow-Teaguer will not fit a Fauxgre will not fit a Giant Cpulba will not fit a Euvyd. Now, Pauline. Can you lift a cinder block?"

Pauline strode over to a mound of blocks, piled three into a small tower, then picked up the whole stack.

"Impressive. Humans are more powerful than they are often given credit for. Can you handle a cement trowel?"

"Tym will teach me. Right, Tym?"

"Of course. Let's get started!"

When all the gas masks had been distributed, Chance went to work on a ladder next to his sister, laying cinder blocks. The barrier was now almost twenty-three feet high, about seventeen to go. Even with all the noise and bustle of the forklifts and backhoes, a terrific rumbling could be heard above them—the vibrations of Valentine's excavators

digging ever closer. Why hadn't he kept his promise? A little more than four hours to go, and the penthouse would be finished and ready for the sealant.

Screeching audio feedback startled the siblings, and Tym nearly fell off his ladder.

"Corps, friends, volunteers," Glandaw said through a bullhorn from atop a ziggurat of cinder blocks on center court. "It's going to be close. Do what you must to redouble your efforts. The good news is that the East Graxanian Contract Bridge Club—twenty Vyrndeets strong—will be here momentarily with their extension ladders to assist in building the penthouse barrier; this should cut thirty minutes off our estimated completion time."

The rumble from the excavators was of such a low frequency it was more felt than heard, and the effect was literally nauseating. Several members of the Corps of Engineers, disabled by nausea, were forced to stop work and lie down on the tennis courts.

Meanwhile a call had gone out to the Bricklayers' Union, and soon volunteers were appearing by the dozens. The problem was a shortage of ladders of sufficient length to reach what would eventually be a forty-foot barrier. A crew of enterprising Yfpostons had taken to lashing together short ladders to make long ones, though they were inherently more dangerous, and only the bravest of bricklayers employed them.

Hours later, Chance and Pauline, bathed in sweat, their arms and legs and backs aching spectacularly, their hands masses of cuts and blisters, each climbed another rung on their respective ladders, reached up, and touched the Donbalese sky. It was slick and cool, and felt truly ancient under their fingertips.

"Just a couple feet to go, Chance," said Pauline. "Gonna make it?"

"You bet," Chance said with more conviction than he felt. Two or three more layers of cinder blocks, then the last layer, each block milled by an engineer to fit perfectly into the space between the top of the barrier and the uneven ceiling, and it would be ready for the sealant.

A half-ton slab of rock, jiggled loose by the vibrations from the excavators, fell into one of the doubles lanes on tennis court 6, narrowly missing a Euvyd mixing cement. Other massive slabs began to fall here and there. Glandaw put herself in charge of watching the sky.

"Pauline, I don't understand why those huge rock chunks aren't just crashing through the tennis courts, leaving gaping holes," said Chance.

"I heard Glandaw talking about a whole crew of creatures whose job it is to reinforce the ceiling of the top floor of the building, from inside. I guess they're doing a pretty good job."

"I think the miners are going to break through before

we finish," Chance said, as they watched another massive slab fall on the roof of the Zek-Chthon. "All this will have been for nothing, and everyone will die."

"Chance, get a hold of yourself. Our job is to build this barrier as fast and expertly as we can, and leave everything else to Glandaw and the Corps."

"And even if we do succeed, the penthouse will essentially be a tomb—no one will be allowed to come or go."

"Chance, don't worry. I've been watching them build a set of air locks to the inside of the building that creatures can pass through. We'll be all right."

A flat, jagged slab of stone came loose from the sky, fell like a guillotine blade through space, and punctured one of the hot-air balloons at the far north end of the developing penthouse. The proprietor of the balloon concession, a skittish Geckasoft, stood there in his gas mask, wringing his hands and looking anxious. Earlier he would occasionally sally out to the bricklayers and shout encouragement. Now he just crouched in a corner and appeared to be praying.

"Last layer, Chance," said Pauline. "It'll take longer because we can't just use any old cinder block. We have to use the exact one we're told to use, the one that has been customized to fit between the top layer and the sky. A big cinder block jigsaw puzzle."

An exhausted Euvyd began climbing Chance's ladder, carrying a misshapen block. She finally reached Chance.

"This is custom block P-181. Mortar it well, and insert with the red arrow up and inside. Okay?"

Chance did as he was told. The block fit perfectly. The Euvyd brought him blocks P-182, P-183, then P-184, and so on. Meanwhile, the sealing process had begun. Creatures with tanks on their backs attached to nozzles were busy spraying sealant over every inch of the barrier.

Then the Euvyd climbed the ladder with block P-200.

"This is the last one, human. Don't waste any time."

Just as Chance began mortaring the last block to complete the barrier of the penthouse, a terrible *krrrlk!* resounded throughout the massive room. Chance turned around to see the ceiling distend like a woofer, then burst. An almost paranormal silence reigned for a few instants while huge slabs of rock, followed by a vast machine, fell through space, landing in a deafening heap on tennis court 4. The hole it left in the sky was thirty feet in diameter if an inch. Almost immediately a torrent of warm air blew through the penthouse, scattering unused cinder blocks, tipping forklifts, knocking creatures off their feet. The swirling mass of air nearly swept Chance off the top of the forty-foot ladder, but he held on and was able to lay the last cinder block before the air pressure destabilized. The room was complete and sealed, the last refuge of a crushed and inoperable Bucyrus RH400 excavator.

Glandaw ordered the operator of the excavator to be rescued. Creatures swarmed the pile of rock and rubble to

free the operator, who was not hurt. Chance and Pauline expected to see Valentine Sleaford himself, but instead a slight man in his fifties emerged.

Glandaw asked him his business.

"I am Riley Stoltz. I am the foreman of the Donbaloh Mining Project. Mr. Valentine Sleaford ordered me to halt the operation, but I disobeyed him. I was committed to his views on the gold economy and decided to continue the project without his approval. He is not to blame."

Riley Stoltz was taken into custody and escorted off the premises.

Chance and Pauline looked up into the thirty-foot hole in the ceiling. It was black as ink, a few twinkling stars the only illumination. The siblings looked at each other.

"Oppabof!"

Silence ruled the penthouse. The air pressure had stabilized, the barrier had been successful at keeping the atmospheres from mixing, the three other Bucyrus RH400 excavators above were inactive, abandoned long ago by their operators. It was now Glandaw's job to fix the hole in the ceiling.

"Chance, how in the world are we going to get out?" said Pauline. "We can't just climb a ladder through the hole, the edges are too steep and jagged."

"I have an idea. Come on!"

Chance bolted for the far north end of the penthouse,

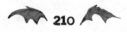

Pauline in swift pursuit. He approached the skittish Geckasoft whose hot-air balloon had been destroyed earlier.

"I am Chance, and I'd like to make you an offer you can't refuse."

"I am Rtlyon Phlange. Since all is lost, I'd like to hear it."

"I would like to purchase one of your balloons. I have sixty thousand clahd."

"Done."

"But you must also make a delivery for me."

"A delivery?"

"You must get this envelope to Prefect Tylotch Plariant."

"Plariant! But . . . but one never knows where he is!"

"Take it to his mother," said Pauline. "At 568.145 Jaulareo Bulster."

Chance handed Rtlyon Phlange his sixty thousand clahd and a sealed envelope with 600,000 clahd more.

"Will you help us launch the balloon?"

"What're you going to do, fly around this big room?"

"No. We want to fly up through that hole in the sky."

Chance, Pauline, and Rtlyon dragged a half-inflated balloon with a green, gold, and purple harlequin pattern over to tennis court 4. Rtlyon fired up the flame, and the balloon slowly began to inflate.

"Okay, climb in the basket, you two!" shouted Rtlyon.

The siblings climbed in, where there was barely enough room for the two of them. Rtlyon dragged the balloon

directly underneath the thirty-foot hole, then cut the anchor. The Jeopards began to slowly ascend.

"Wait! Eton!"

Rtlyon leaped and grabbed hold of the basket, pulling it back down with his body weight. Meanwhile, Glandaw came running up, Eton in her arms. She hoisted him up and in.

"Good-bye, Glandaw!"

"I'll miss you!" came a voice from behind them. They turned to see Braig and Tym waving furiously.

"Bye, you guys!"

The balloon floated through the hole, a very snug fit, and into the widening gyre of the mining pit. Before long they were level with the Earth, where a pastel sunrise was coloring the east.

"Look!" said Pauline, pointing to the horizon as they rose ever higher. There, on the edge of the pit, stood a single-wide trailer. Standing in front of it was a tiny figure, waving.

"Valentine Sleaford!" said Chance.

"He tried to stop it," said Pauline. "Let's give him that."

The prevailing winds began to push the balloon toward the east. Chance and Pauline were exhausted, and both fell asleep standing up. When they woke, five hours later, they were thousands of feet above the ground, and neither had any idea where they were. They'd had nothing to eat or drink in ages, the midmorning sun was beating down on them, and they had absolutely no control over the direction

of the balloon. They could effect its altitude by regulating the amount of heat produced by the flame, but that was all. They just had to hope they were heading home.

Off in the distance Chance noticed a huge water tower. On it was stenciled the word CHAMBERLAIN, the name of a town not far from Starling.

"We're headed in the right direction, Chance!" exclaimed Pauline. "How easily we could have floated to Mexico or Oklahoma. I think we should set this bird down."

Chance cut the fuel to the flame, and it extinguished. The balloon began to slowly lose altitude.

"I'm going to try to contact Mersey."

Pauline removed her fulgurite necklace from her sock and placed it around her neck.

Mersey?

Pauline! Where are you?

Mersey, Donbaloh is saved! We're out, and we're in a hot-air balloon. I have Chance with me. It looks like we're going to land about half a mile south of Chamberlain, near a fork in a river. The Chamberlain water tower is north-northwest of our position, we'll head toward it. Can you come and get us?"

On my way.

Bring changes of clothes, food, and water.

Done.

The basket of the balloon hit the ground, hard, and threw Eton and the siblings free. The wind carried it off to the east, the basket dragging through the scrub oak and

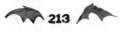

mesquite. It was midafternoon, another scorcher, at least 110 degrees. The trio began walking toward the water tower, more than half a mile distant. Eventually they came to a road heading toward town. Cars and trucks raced past them, some slowing to get a better look at Pauline, who was still dressed in a kind of royal blue velveteen cape.

Then, in the distance, a battered old green Ford F-150 appeared in the southbound lane. It slowed next to them, and the driver's-side window rolled down.

Mersey. Her makeup was streaked with tears.

"Wow, am I glad to see you two."

Eton began barking, bearing witness to himself.

"And this must be Eton."

Pauline and Chance were so tired all they could do was smile and climb in the cab of the pickup and fall immediately asleep.

Mersey drove them home. Mercifully, the siblings' mother happened to be out. They each went to their respective rooms and climbed into bed.

CHAPTER 28

Fallor Medoby Dox sat in his chair at his escritoire, dozing, waiting for FedEx to deliver a recent major acquisition: L. Frank Baum's *The Wizard of Oz*, a fine first edition with dust jacket, both the binding and text in their first state, purchased from Timbeau Rare Books of London. It would be a superb addition to his collection of works featuring humans capable of taking flight. (Among the inventory of humans, Fallor counted witches.) Except the FedEx deliverywoman was running late today: Urszula had yet to make an appearance.

Outside his window two birds, a red-billed chough and

a great spotted woodpecker, occupied an aspen bough, seemingly at ease. Fallor wondered why they were not bothered by each other, why one did not fly off. It was warm for Gstaad today; perhaps they were simply happy in the shade of the canopy, content to coexist. Fallor loved birds. Next to books, they were his essential passion. If—

A rap at the door. Fallor recognized it immediately: Urszula.

"Good day, my dear. Have you a parcel from London for me?"

"Not today, Fallor. Today you have been addressed by an individual from a town in Texas in the United States of America. A slender envelope only—no books concealed within, I'm afraid. Sign here."

Fallor had been wondering if he would hear from Chance Jeopard. He sat in his easy chair and slit open the envelope. Inside was a single sheet of paper, folded twice.

Dear Mr. Medoby Dox,
I am happy to report that Donbaloh is safe. The mining company succeeded in breaking through, but with the reluctant assistance of Tylotch Plariant the breach was contained and the atmospheres did not mingle. My sister and I have since been out to the mining site, and it has been filled in. The miners themselves, including their leader, Valentine Sleaford, have all been

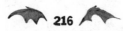

sworn to secrecy. The miner who broke through is still in Donbaloh; he was not hurt, but his fate is unknown.

Thank you for all of your assistance; my sister, Pauline, and I could never have made it without your help.

Sincerely yours,
Chance B. Jeopard

Fallor had never really stopped to consider what would happen if Donbaloh were exposed to Oppabof. The destruction would be unprecedented in the twenty-first century. Countless lives lost, and total plunder of her mineral resources.

Fallor wished he could meet these young people, Chance and Pauline, and express his gratitude. He moved to his escritoire and sat, arranging his wing so that it was out of his way. He dipped his pen in the inkwell—only the finest iron-gall ink—and withdrew a sheet of the best hand-made foolscap.

He began to compose a letter.

CHAPTER 29

August thirty-first. Chance, Mersey, and Pauline just returned from delivering Eton to his owner in Buda, Texas. The night before Chance had put the finishing touches on his graphic novelization of his and his sister's adventures in Donbaloh. This time he was not afraid to show the finished product to Mersey and his sister.

"Oh, how I wish I'd been there," said Mersey, sitting cross-legged on a throw rug in Pauline's room, flipping through Chance's book. "I could have been of some assistance."

"You were miraculous aboveground," said Pauline. "You actually *stopped* Valentine Sleaford."

"But I couldn't stop the rogue miner."

"That's the definition of 'rogue,' I think," said Chance. "Unstoppable."

"I wonder what happened to him," said Pauline.

A knock at the door.

"Hi, guys. Can I come in?"

"Sure!"

"Hands are full, a little help with the door."

Chance let his mother in. She was carrying a tray with three Arnold Palmers, a bag of corn chips, and a bowl of salsa.

"Wow! Thanks!"

Pauline had been worried about her mother. She had never again heard from Fred Antaso; he had just disappeared. How she was dying to tell her mother Fred's true story, but of course she could not. Daisy had always played her cards close to the vest, even when their father had died, but there was no way she was not hurting. Daisy channeled all her negative emotions into yoga, and she emerged every day stronger than ever. Pauline had occasionally considered taking up the discipline. Maybe now was the time.

Chance was worried about his mother, too. Her heart *must* have been broken, but she did not show it. No one had spoken about Fred since they'd come back from Donbaloh in mid-August—Fred was conspicuous by his very absence.

"Mom, whatever happened to Fred?"

Pauline and Mersey froze, stared at each other. Daisy

put the tray down on Pauline's desk, smoothly, without a hitch or start. She stood up, pushed her hair out of her eyes, and smiled.

"I got a note from Fred. He told me he had experienced a great enlightenment, and that he had always loved me and my whole family, but that I would not see him again. He wished us all well. You too, Mersey."

Chance thought he saw a glistening in his mother's eye but could not be sure. She turned and left, closing the door quietly behind her.

Pauline, Chance, and Mersey said nothing. They sat still in the afternoon silence for a long time. Eventually, Pauline stood up and distributed the Arnold Palmers all around. They finished the chips and salsa, each thinking hard about the events of a few weeks earlier.

Another knock on the door.

"Me again. FedEx for Chance. From Switzerland!"

After Daisy left, Chance tore open the envelope. He read aloud:

Dear Chance and Pauline Jeopard,
Thank you for your note, which came as a great relief. I cannot imagine the trials you must have endured navigating your way around Donbaloh as humans, and I am astonished that you were able to intersect with Tylotch Plariant. I am glad you are

safely home, and thank you for your service to the Realm.

Most cordial regards,
Fallor M. Dox

Chance folded the letter in half, then in half again. When he had a moment to himself, he would add it to his graphic novel, where it would form the last page.

The first time Pauline and Chance had made it safely home from Donbaloh, back at the beginning of the summer, a grand thunderstorm had gathered in the west. They had all watched it from the picture window, a magnificent, thundering and flashing coda to their adventure.

Pauline and Chance and Mersey gazed out the picture window again, looking for signs of a storm.

But only the shimmer of the white heat of Starling, Texas, bore down on the plains before them.

APPENDIX

DONBALESE FLORA AND FAUNA
MENTIONED IN THE TEXT

BALLIOPE: Short, spherical beast with long antennae and a taste for law and order. Common. As a species they form the infantry of Donbaloh's security forces, with headquarters on the 3023rd floor of Saint Philomene's Infirmary. Sleeps a lot.

CHARL: Adorable, furry three-legged creature with the extraordinary ability to hum, mezzo-soprano, complex melodies of its own devising. Popular as pets, though given to malaise and grumpiness.

CLINGING HASPLE: A creature of great intelligence and ethics, a Hasple is similar in appearance to a dragonfly, if that dragonfly were a foot long with hands of significant crushing power. Allergic to everything.

COCHLIQUE: Flightless duck-like creature with two tiny heads that converse with each other and often argue or call each other names. Once exploited by circuses and side-shows. Rare and desirable as pets.

DANDELICT: Comely creature with leonine features and strange, helical tendrils of "hair" growing from its head. Intelligent and thoughtful, but tends to dissolve into pure id when discussing politics. Donbaloh's greatest numismatists have all been Dandelicts.

DELECTA MAKINDEE: A voracious, beetle-like insect that feeds only on decaying flesh. A colony can skeletonize a Balliope in minutes. Baked and dipped in cheese, it is a Donbalese delicacy.

DEWPIE: Snake-like creature that exudes a sugary film when agitated; this film has an agreeable violet taste and can be licked off the dewpie. By virtue of this, they make great pets for children, though licking one's dewpie more than once a day is not recommended.

DOJIMOBI: A curious wild beast distantly related to the Oppaboffian reebok, long ago raised for meat. Now only

Dojimobis that die naturally are considered fit for consumption, but they must be immediately dressed. Their rib-eye cutlets are prized.

ERIG-BABST: Highly curious and investigative creature organized a bit like a dog and an aardvark. Somewhat dim-witted. Loyal as pets, terrible as guard creatures due to their long and profound sleep cycle.

EUVYD: Similar to the human in appearance, but biologically unrelated. Identifiable by bright blue, sticking-out ears, clear hair, and forehead tattoos of obscure meaning. Gregarious and fearless. Commonly found working in libraries and bookstores. Were once the only link to Oppabof, where they labored as customs agents for imports and exports.

FAUXGRE: An intimidating beast and ogre look-alike, the fauxgre has little in common with the true ogre, save great strength. It is a serene, sleepy being of some mental limitation. Most of the species work as bookbinders, printers, or stand-up comedians.

FEMMA-THLADROOK: Tall, strong creature resembling a cross between an abominable snowman and a mailbox. Employed in the fiduciary disciplines such as the administration of tax advice and general accounting. Femma-Thladreek (pl.) share a collective psyche and can

tackle highly complex problems by pooling their powers of intellect.

FLENTH-ON-THE-COB: A very sweet vegetable eaten like corn-on-the-cob, though the "cob," when roasted and split open, reveals a syrupy marrow used as a base for salad dressings.

FYLARIA-LIT: A sturdily built creature related in appearance to the superhero Conan the Barbarian, but with a slender neck and delicate features. Unfailingly loyal, the Fylaria-Lit make very good friends. Often employed in the field of bodyguarding, though a fair percentage have done well in the funerary arts.

GECKASOFT: An intelligent creature not unlike the Oppaboffian film star E.T. in appearance, but delicate and slender. Known for its sharp wit, bad breath, and an unfortunate biological magnetism to virtually any disease. Powerfully magical, it is sometimes the last resort for doctors confronted with otherwise incurable diseases, yet a Geckasoft cannot treat itself. Fine chess and Go player.

GIANT CPULBA: Lovable, roundish furry creature that travels by hopping. Susceptible to tricks and pranks. Teenage Cpulba tend toward shyness and nerdiness but become sociable and cuddly when mature. Can be fierce when committed to a cause. Usually finds employment as an ocular surgeon.

HARROW-TEAGUER: Twenty-foot colossus covered in black wood-like scales, its arms each ending in two powerful phalanges that can pinch a garbage can flat. Tidy dresser, gambling issues, superstitious. There are no females; a Harrow-Teaguer reproduces by chopping off the end of its tail and placing it in a dish of ice water.

HIGLEY: Resembles a large, leather tuning fork, the two "legs" of which terminate in small three-legged stools. Higley always travel in pairs. Slightly paranoid, and often disseminates conspiracy theories. Marvelous cooks, invented Higley sauce, a piquant base of certain marinades.

KENICKI-QUITHER: Enormous, furry, lumbering creature sometimes kept as a pet by Harrow-Teaguers. Pleasant-smelling and polite, the Kenicki-Quither makes its home in the many Donbalese parks and arboreta, where it works as a soothsayer. Occasional victim of the Outsize Zampoglio Weed.

LESSER WHOOK (PL. WHEEK): Graceful, playful winged creature resembling a dove crossed with a paper airplane. Lives exclusively in Middlespace at Saint Philomene's Infirmary. Once used as a messenger. The Greater Whook is long extinct, though there are two Middling Wheek in captivity, refusing to mate.

MANTLE RAT: An almost mythically hideous creature not unlike a miniature black bear with long spidery legs.

Scurries along the catacombs and basements eating whatever it sees. Well-dressed, reportedly telepathic, lives to a great old age.

PACIFICA GOZO: Winged humanoid creature of great probity. Half its population migrated to Oppabof in the 1630s, living among humans. It can fold up its great gossamer wings so they are virtually undetectable under heavy clothes. Great readers: It is estimated that one quarter to one third of all librarians in the eighteenth century were Pacifica Gozo masquerading as humans. Now there are but two remaining in Oppabof.

PEARL BIGNOL: Glassy, spherical being no larger than a marble covered in microscopic legs with which it propels itself along the ground. Venomous to all creatures but Harrow-Teaguers, unless properly cooked in hadulous reduction butter, where they form a pleasant, fragrant sauce.

PLINGE: Poky, turtle-like creature covered in sable-soft fur. Always cold and seeks warmth from other creatures by cuddling. Popular pet among the wealthy and the lonesome.

POPSES: Fleet beast prized for its flavorful meat. Very difficult to catch. Popses T-bones can sell for as much as one thousand clahd per pound. As per law in Donbaloh, no beast can be killed for its meat; it must die a natural death and then may be consumed. The best cuts are taken within minutes of its death, so other creatures are employed

to constantly watch the Popses and other game beasts, in hopes of catching one ready to expire.

QUILPHEKE: Tiny creature similar in appearance to an Oppaboffian hamster, but furless and tailless. Capable of carrying on simple conversations about the weather, television programming, and movie star antics. Concepts such as irony, satire, and absurdity are incomprehensible to the Quilpheke, so can't take a joke.

RECAPHREY: Small, muscular, dragon-like beast with a mule's hindquarters. The Recaphrey has a monopoly on the rickshaw concession in Donbaloh due to its prodigious memory: It is the only creature capable of recalling hundreds of thousands of addresses, and perforce able to pass the Rickshaw Operators Test, the most difficult of all Donbalese civil service examinations.

TERRA HUZZI: A tame but timid creature from Outer Terbolontz, a distant underworld region located roughly beneath Boise, Idaho. When scratched behind the ear, exudes a pheromone that induces a sense of peace and tranquility in the scratcher. Highly sought after by psychiatrists and others in the mind-healing professions. Short-lived and extremely rare.

THROPINESE: Strange creature not unlike a dog-sized beetle dressed for aerobics. Hyperactive mucosal glands. Flatterer. Rather simple. Females of the species are

extremely rare; in desperation, males will woo females of other species. Loves parties.

ULT THIVISH: A selfish, cowardly, venal creature given to gourmandizing and argument. Prospers in politics and high finance. Uncommon in Donbaloh, and growing rarer.

UPRIGHT EYELEIGH: Cute gecko-like creature with big eyes. Looks like it's always smiling. One out of ten thousand can grow wings just by wishing for them. Its cousin, the Recumbent Eyeleigh, has been extinct for hundreds of years.

VALKMANNON: A Donbalese tree prized for its root, which, when dried and ground, has a pleasant, smoky-spicy taste that forms the base of most barbecue sauces.

VLAANDER: A vine cultivated for its bittersweet beans. In olden times thought to have magical properties, and that eating as many Vlaander beans as one could tolerate, then eating one more, would restore an infirm creature to health. Seasonal.

VYRNDEET: Comically structured beast nearly ten feet tall. Employed in menial positions throughout Donbaloh. Suffers from chronic fatigue and sociopathy. Smells like low tide.

WELFT: Delicate plant that grows parasitically on Zampoglio weeds. Its leaves, when dried at the proper

temperature, can be brewed into a fragrant tea that in olden times was used to ease digestion in many species.

WREAU: Well-respected, five-foot creature not unlike a shaved meerkat. Impeccable dresser, clever, a penchant for the stage. Particularly agile representatives of the species often chosen as cheerleaders for various sporting contests.

YFPOSTON: Cerebral creature resembling a steamer trunk upholstered in feathers. Fiercely dedicated to the printed word, they are often employed as librarians, book dealers, or bibliographers. Outwardly genderless, though male, female, and transgender Yfposton can tell one another apart.

ZAMPOGLIO WEED (DIMINUTIVE, INTER-MEDIATE, AND OUTSIZE): Tree outfitted with large snares for catching prey. Dissolves captives in a powerful acid, then drinks it like a martini, pouring it into mouth hidden high in its trunk. Diminutives can pull their roots up and run for short distances; Intermediates are endangered; Outsizes are the fourth-largest organic structures on (or in) planet Earth, after the honey fungus colony, the quaking aspen colony, and the blue whale.

ACKNOWLEDGMENTS

I am deeply grateful for the consistent support and tireless cheerleading of the following people: Philippe Aronson, Allene Cassagnol, Marcio Coello, Bob and Cathy Cotter, Albert Cotton III, Melissa and Brian Dempsey, Liz Dresner, Adam Eaglin, Karen and Joe Etherton, Jennifer Fahrenbacher, Pansy and Elliott Flick, Laura Godwin, Nancy Gore, Jackie and Rob Kelly, Sara Kocek, Karen Krajcer, Michael Laird, Lelia Mander, Isabel Mendía, Rachel Murray, Carly Nelson, John Norris, Lenka Norris, Sam Ramos, Bryan Sansone, Red Nose Studio, REYoung, and Melisa Vuong.